# Secret at Mystic Lake

# Nancy Drew DIARIES™

Secret at Mystic Lake

#6

CAROLYN KEENE

Aladdin

NEW YORK   LONDON   TORONTO   SYDNEY   NEW DELHI

ALADDIN

An imprint of Simon & Schuster Children's Publishing Division

1230 Avenue of the Americas, New York, NY 10020

First Aladdin paperback edition May 2014

Text copyright © 2014 by Simon & Schuster, Inc.

Cover illustration copyright © 2014 by Erin McGuire

All rights reserved, including the right of reproduction in whole or in part in any form.

ALADDIN is a trademark of Simon & Schuster, Inc., and related logo is a registered trademark of Simon & Schuster, Inc.

NANCY DREW, NANCY DREW DIARIES, and related logo are trademarks of Simon & Schuster, Inc.

Also available in an Aladdin hardcover edition.

For information about special discounts for bulk purchases, please contact Simon & Schuster Special Sales at 1-866-506-1949 or business@simonandschuster.com.

The Simon & Schuster Speakers Bureau can bring authors to your live event. For more information or to book an event contact the Simon & Schuster Speakers Bureau at 1-866-248-3049 or visit our website at www.simonspeakers.com.

Cover designed by Karin Paprocki

Interior designed by Karina Granda

The text of this book was set in Adobe Caslon Pro.

Manufactured in the United States of America 0719 OFF

10

Library of Congress Control Number 2013951023

ISBN 978-1-4814-0012-1 (pbk)

ISBN 978-1-4814-0013-8 (hc)

ISBN 978-1-4814-0014-5 (eBook)

# Contents

## Dear Diary,

**HOW MUCH BAD LUCK CAN YOU HAVE ON ONE TRIP?**

That's the question I've been asking myself ever since George, Bess, and I left on a bike tour around the beautiful Mystic Lake Park. What we thought would be a chance to take in some scenery and bond with nature has been nothing but disaster. Our tents were stolen, we were drenched in a nighttime downpour, and our food disappeared. And we've only been gone for twenty-four hours!

Now I'm starting to think that someone's out to sabotage the tour.

It couldn't be one of our fellow cyclists. Could it?

# CHAPTER ONE

◈

# Just One Small Problem

"I CAN'T BELIEVE I'M DOING THIS," MY FRIEND
Bess Marvin muttered, poking morosely at her eggs.

George Fayne, my other friend and Bess's cousin,
elbowed her and grinned. "It's because you love me so
much," she said. "Just remember that."

We were all eating breakfast at the quaint inn
where our upcoming three-day bike tour around the
scenic, sprawling Mystic Lake Park was about to start.

George's parents had bought the trip for all three of us as a birthday gift to George, and they'd come to drop us off so we wouldn't have to leave our cars. Bess wasn't exactly as thrilled about the trip as George and I were. In fact, she was distinctly unthrilled.

"It'll be good for you, Bess," Mr. Fayne said. "Get out of town for a few days. Get back to nature. Get some exercise. . . ."

Bess sighed and looked balefully at her cousin. "Why can't you be really into outlet shopping?" she asked. "Why can't your most dearly held birthday wish be, like, sitting on a beach in Saint Thomas for three days?"

George shook her head. "Because I'm not you?" she retorted. "Come on, Bess. This will be fun. I bet you'll end up loving it." Though they were related, Bess and George couldn't be more different from each other. George was sharp, sensible, and outdoorsy; Bess was cheerful, fashionable, and decidedly not outdoorsy.

"Like I've been loving all our practice rides?" Bess asked snarkily, then couldn't help breaking into a smile. George and I both started laughing.

"Come on, Bess," I said, gently nudging her. "You only cried for the first hour last time!"

The truth was that Bess had been a pretty good sport on the practice rides the three of us had taken around our hometown of River Heights. We'd started at ten miles and worked our way up to thirty-five, which was the length of the rides we'd be taking on the tour. I was no athlete, but I kind of liked the bike rides; it was exhilarating whooshing through the town, almost like you were flying. I'd been sore for days after the first couple of rides, but gradually I'd gotten stronger. After our last ride, I hadn't had to take even one aspirin.

"Ooh, look," said George, pointing at a tall, honey-blond girl who'd just stepped into the dining room. She was wearing bike shorts and a slim tank top, and her hair was pulled back into a sleek low ponytail. Behind her came a boy about her age, also with honey-blond hair, but his was cut short and matched the stubble on his face and chin. He wore a pair of cargo shorts and a baggy T-shirt that read A LEGEND IN MY OWN TIME. "I think that's Caitlin and Henry—they're twins, and they're leading the tour." Our tour was run by a business called Adventures & Company that George said ran lots of these types of trips, but Caitlin and Henry had been featured online as the coleaders of our particular trek.

Caitlin smiled and headed toward us, gesturing for Henry, who looked less enthusiastic, to follow. "Hi, I'm Caitlin Moorehead. Are you all here for the bike tour?"

"We are," said Bess, standing and offering her hand. "I'm Bess Marvin, and this is my cousin George Fayne and my friend Nancy Drew."

Caitlin and Henry shook each of our hands. "Welcome," said Caitlin. "I think we're going to have a lot of fun." She smiled, but I couldn't help noticing that there was something tense behind her smile.

Then again, maybe I was reading too much into it. I have a tendency to do that sometimes. See, my thing is solving mysteries. My friends love to tease me about it, but they're always happy to join me in cracking a case. Together we've snagged more than our fair share of crooks in River Heights.

If there was something odd in Caitlin's expression, Mr. Fayne didn't seem to notice. "I'm Russ Fayne, George's dad," he said.

"Nice to meet you," Caitlin said, shaking his hand. "It's beautiful up here, isn't it?"

Mr. Fayne smiled, but his expression quickly turned serious. "And what are the safety procedures on a trip like this?" he asked. "What if, for example, there were an emergency?"

Caitlin nodded, looking unruffled. "Well, I'll always have my satellite phone with me, so we can contact emergency services even when we can't get cell service," she said. The website for the tour had made it very clear: There was little, if any, cell service in the Mystic Lake region. "But I've also taken several courses in first aid, including CPR and child CPR. And I carry a full first aid kit, of course." She paused, then flashed that same tense smile. "I've been a cyclist on at least ten of these trips, though, sir, and nothing's ever gone wrong beyond some bumps and bruises. I wouldn't worry too much!"

Mr. Fayne didn't smile. "And what is your background?" he asked. "How does one become qualified to give a tour like this?"

Again, Caitlin didn't seem bothered in the least as she launched into a description of how she'd grown up doing long-distance biking trips with her parents, camped all over the country, was a varsity athlete in high school, and was planning to study environmental science at Yale in the fall.

"Yale?" George asked, her eyebrows raised. "Wow, that's impressive."

Henry smirked. "My sis is too modest to tell you, but she's going on a full merit scholarship from Grayson Industries, a biotech firm in our town," he put in. "She beat out loads of impressive candidates with her 4.5 GPA!"

Even Bess looked impressed by that. "How did you get higher than a 4.0?" she asked Caitlin. "Isn't that the best GPA you can get?"

Caitlin rolled her eyes, looking embarrassed. "It's the way our school counts advanced placement courses," she said. "You get some extra points. No big deal."

But Bess still looked puzzled, as though she was trying to do the math in her head. "How many AP courses did you take?" she asked.

Caitlin was turning slightly pink. "Eight," she replied quietly.

"Wow," Bess said breathlessly, shaking her head. "Well, I guess I should feel confident putting my life in your hands!"

She turned to Henry. "What about you?" she asked. "You're coleading the ride, aren't you?"

Henry gave her an easy grin. "I am. But only because the tour company insists on having two people lead, if they're under twenty-one. And it makes my parents happy, honestly. Caitlin's done most of the planning. She's the overachiever in the family. For instance, while Cait's up pulling all-nighters next year, I'll be relaxing in the south of France!" He elbowed his sister. "I'm taking a year off to travel."

Henry smiled as he said that, I noted, but Caitlin didn't. She turned back to us, all business.

"Are there any other questions I can answer for you guys?"

As Mr. Fayne interrogated Caitlin and Henry some more, George reached over and touched my arm. "Let's make sure we have all our gear together," she suggested.

"Sure," I agreed, and got up from the table to follow her and Bess out to the foyer, where we'd placed our packs.

We each had a large backpack containing a few extra clothes, changes of underwear, toiletries, aspirin—the bare essentials. Caitlin and Henry had provided a list of items we'd need for the trip, but they didn't include too much. "Probably so we don't get bogged down with stuff during the ride," George had noted happily. We all also carried a big bottle of water, and George's parents had gotten us some protein bars, "just in case." (Meals were included in the tour, but the Faynes didn't want us to get hungry.) The Faynes had also sprung for a super-fancy, superlight tent that the three of us would take turns carrying on the rides and share at night. It was separate from the packs, and George suggested that we draw straws to figure out who would take it first. I "won," so I would carry it on the first leg of our trip, until lunch today.

As George and I peeked outside, where our tour-issued bikes were waiting, Bess sauntered up to us, took one look at the packs, and shook her head. "I hope you know," she said, "that this is by far the most outdoorsy thing I have ever done."

"OMG, me too!" a female, slightly nasal voice piped up from the top of the stairs, and we looked up to see a curly-haired brunette with startling blue eyes walking down, carrying a huge backpack and tent. "Are you guys leaving on the tour?"

"We sure are," George said, smiling. "We're really excited. I'm George, and this is Bess and Nancy. You are . . . ?"

The girl smiled, revealing a slightly crooked bottom tooth. "I'm Zoe. Zoe Ferullo. Gosh, I'm so glad to meet you guys. I don't know anyone on this tour—I signed up to go with my friend Gemma, who is totally outdoorsy, but then she backed out at the last minute. She got mono." She paused, looked off to the side, and smiled wickedly. "I told her that would only make her as lazy as I am, but she wasn't buying it! Haw, haw, haw, haw."

Zoe bent over laughing at her own joke, and Bess giggled too.

"Girls?"

We all looked up to see George's parents approaching the doorway from the breakfast room, already getting misty-eyed.

"It's about time to get going," Mr. Fayne said, walking over to George and putting an arm around her shoulders.

I smiled at him. "Caitlin and Henry passed your interrogation?"

Mr. Fayne nodded and smiled. "Just be happy you have Georgia's mother and me looking out for you girls."

George winced at the sound of her real name. Nobody ever used it except for her parents. But she quickly recovered and leaned in to give him a hug. "Oh, we are," she assured him.

Caitlin and Henry appeared in the doorway then. Henry looked relaxed as he checked his phone, but Caitlin looked slightly stressed. She put on a bright smile and said, "Bike tour participants, I have to apologize. We had a printer malfunction last night"—here she shot Henry a meaningful glance—"and I was unable to print out your tour maps. But Henry and I have maps, and I promise you're safe under our leadership!"

Zoe laughed that awful laugh. "Haw, haw. What would a map even have on it out here—'You pass more trees here, then more trees'?"

George cleared her throat. "I think what Zoe means is . . . it's fine," she said, shooting Caitlin a comforting smile.

Caitlin's grin seemed to become a little more relaxed then. "Great. Well, let's all go outside. It's time to get ready to roll!"

Twenty minutes later I settled myself on my bike seat and pushed off, following behind Bess, George, and four others, including Zoe.

The Faynes stood waving on the steps of the bed-and-breakfast.

"Have fun!" Mrs. Fayne called. Bess turned around and shook her head as if to say, *Like that's possible.*

George turned her head and flashed a sincere smile at her parents. "Thank you so much, you guys!"

We all kept waving and calling our good-byes until we rounded a corner out of sight. We passed a low wall of pine trees and suddenly a gorgeous vista came into view: rolling hills surrounding a glimmering blue lake. Mystic Lake. Everyone oohed and aahed.

Henry, who was in the lead with Caitlin, turned his head to call back, "This is just the beginning! You guys won't believe the beauty we'll experience on this trip."

Bess, who was already panting behind me, let out a little sigh. "I hope we experience lots of resting, too," she muttered, too low for most of the group to hear. But Zoe, who was in the back of the pack with us, laughed that same crazy laugh.

"Haw, haw, haw, haw! You said it. This is pretty

and all, but I'd be just as happy at home in front of last night's *Project Runway*."

Bess glanced at Zoe with a surprised, wide-eyed stare that said something like, *You just might be my soul mate.* "Who's your favorite?" she asked, tossing her long blond ponytail.

"Angelo," Zoe replied quickly. "Heather is too avant-garde for me. And Justin can only do pants."

Bess nodded appreciatively. "Oh my gosh, come ride by me," she said, gesturing to the space next to her bike. "You could be the one thing that gets me through this tour."

I couldn't help smiling—trust Bess to find a fellow fashionista and outdoors-hater, even in the least likely of places. But then I caught George's eye as Bess pedaled ahead, making space for Zoe.

She gave me a skeptical look. "Figures," she whispered. "I finally get Bess out of the mall, and she finds a fellow shopper."

By the time we stopped at a still green pond for lunch, we'd seen a family of deer, two groundhogs, a bald eagle, and something George swore was an elk but just looked like a big log to me. We'd also seen, as Henry had promised, tons more breathtaking scenery.

Still, I could feel my muscles complaining as I dragged myself off the bike and walked the short distance from where we'd left our gear by the side of the road to the picnic tables a few yards through the trees, by the pond. *It's going to be an aspirin night!* I thought.

George took in the clear, still pond, ringed by wildflowers, with a towering purple hill in the distance, and let out an appreciative sigh. "Isn't it amazing?" she asked. "This is exactly what I was dreaming of when I told my parents about this tour."

A short, gray-haired man beside her, one of our fellow bikers, looked out at the same vista and nodded sagely. "Communing with nature makes us feel more alive," he said solemnly.

George looked over at him and smiled. "I don't know if we've met. I'm George," she said.

"Dagger," he replied, nodding.

"And I'm Nancy," I added.

"Nice to meet you both."

Dagger was the only person on the tour we hadn't yet met. The group was made up of Bess, George, myself, Henry, Caitlin, Zoe, and Dagger. So far Dagger, Caitlin, and Henry seemed like serious bikers, while George, Bess, Zoe, and I pulled up the rear. Caitlin was very patient with us, though. She pointed out that we were all there to see the sights, first and foremost—how fast we saw them was unimportant.

We all settled down by the pond while Caitlin fished around in a cooler and brought out sandwiches and fruit. Henry walked up to the table and sat down heavily. I noticed he made no move to help his sister, who arranged eight sandwiches on the table, all in color-coded plastic bags.

"The red are ham and cheese, the green are turkey with lettuce and tomato, and the yellow are hummus and cucumber," she said, smiling sheepishly. "I didn't know if we had any vegetarians or vegans in the group."

"No animal products for me! I'm vegan, and I'm

starving," Dagger said, reaching for a yellow bag. "Thanks!"

Bess seemed restless; she kept glancing back at the road with an uncomfortable expression on her face.

"Something wrong, cuz?" George asked, taking a big bite of her ham and cheese sandwich.

Bess grimaced. "It's just—is it really safe to leave our stuff by the side of the road like that?" she asked. "I know we're in the middle of nowhere, but it feels wrong."

Caitlin laughed. "We're in a beautiful, rustic spot— not quite the middle of nowhere," she said, gesturing to the pond. "Would nowhere have scenery like this?"

Bess looked unamused. "It's very pretty," she said, "but you know what I mean."

Zoe spoke up. "It feels a little weird to me, too, Bess—it must be a city girl thing!"

George glanced at me and rolled her eyes. *We're all city girls,* she mouthed.

Zoe went on, "But who's going to take our stuff out here?"

Henry nodded. "Exactly—it's totally safe, guys. If anyone happens by, it will be another hiker who knows how precious that gear is. They'd never steal."

Bess shrugged. "Okay—if you say so." She sat down and we all dug in to our sandwiches, making polite conversation about where we were from, what we did, and what had brought us to the tour. Dagger was a bookkeeper from Chicago who wanted to feel closer to nature, and offered to lead us all in meditation just after dawn the next morning. Henry and Caitlin were recent high school graduates from the nearby town of Taylorville. Zoe was a college student who was spending the summer with her parents in nearby Cedar Village.

"I only came on this tour," she said, dramatically waving her orange section, "because my friend Gemma made me."

Caitlin raised an eyebrow. "Oh, great," she said. If she was being sarcastic, Zoe didn't pick up on it.

"I'm really not a nature person," she went on. "I like comfy beds, and good sheets, and manicures, and cable TV. But Adventures and Company said my deposit was nonrefundable, so I'm doing my best to be a good sport. Like, I brought a ton of nail polish, so if anyone wants a manicure tonight, you know where to go."

Bess raised her hand. "Me!" she said cheerfully. "I want a manicure tonight."

Zoe smirked at her. "We can complain to each other about all the good TV we're missing."

Caitlin bunched up her lunch bag with a loud crinkling sound. "Anyway," she said, "we have another twenty miles or so before we get to our campsite, so we'd better get going."

Everyone stood, and when I struggled to get to my feet, I fully realized how stiff my muscles had gotten during our short rest—and how sore I would be that night. Oh well. I was really enjoying the ride and the scenery so far. Caitlin led the way through the trees back to our bikes and gear, but stopped short when she got to the road. "Oh . . . oh no," she murmured.

"What is it?" Zoe asked, crashing through the trees behind her. "Is something wrong?"

Caitlin was staring at the ground. "That's strange,"

she said, turning to look at Henry with a confused expression.

"What?" Zoe asked again.

Henry looked where Caitlin was staring, and his face paled. "Uh—it looks like . . . ?" he said, glancing at his sister.

"Exactly," she said to him. "Weird, no?"

Bess held up a hand, like she was in class. "Can someone please tell me what's wrong?" she asked.

Henry turned to her, clearly trying to look calm. "Oh, it's no biggie," he said, adding in a tense chuckle. "It's just . . . one small problem . . ."

Caitlin shook her head, then pointed at our packs—where, I noticed suddenly, there seemed to be slightly less gear than there was before.

"A bunch of our stuff is gone," she said in a hollow voice. "It looks like . . . our tents are all missing."

~

# CHAPTER TWO

# Back to Nature

ZOE PUSHED HER WAY FORWARD, SHOVING Caitlin aside to take in the empty spot where our tents had been. "Our tents are missing?" she asked. "Are you kidding?"

Caitlin looked pained. "I mean . . . I'm pretty sure they were all right here."

Zoe moved forward and started pushing aside the backpacks, peering around like the tents might be underneath. "Who would steal our tents?"

Henry moved forward to join her and Caitlin, poking at the backpacks and furrowing his brow. "I . . . hmmm."

Bess cleared her throat behind me. "Should we go back?" she asked.

"No!" Caitlin replied, turning to frown at Bess, at the same time as her brother murmured, "Well . . ."

But I was still focused on the *what*, not the *what now*. "Can we go back to Zoe's question?" I asked. "Who would take our tents? It's not like they were that far away, and it's pretty quiet around here. But I didn't hear anyone come up while we were eating."

George nodded. "Yeah—and it's not like this is an easy spot to get to. To get to our stuff without us hearing, a person would have to be on foot. But I guess, on foot, they couldn't have gotten very far."

Henry raised an eyebrow. "That's a good point. Maybe this is a prank."

For some reason this made Caitlin turn to him with an exasperated look. "A prank? Henry, if you—"

But Henry cut her off by raising a hand. "I had nothing to do with it, I swear. I'm just saying, that makes a lot more sense than any other explanation I can think of." He gestured back to the rest of us, still standing in the trees. "We didn't hear anybody ride or hike up. But each of us left the group at one point to use the bathroom or get supplies."

We all looked at one another uncomfortably. He was saying one of us took the tents. Awk-ward.

Caitlin seemed to consider his words, then looked back at us, her charges. One by one, she looked us in the eye and seemed to mentally calculate our likelihood of being behind a tent-stealing prank. "Okay," she said finally, in a clipped, no-nonsense voice. "Let's spread out and take ten minutes to look for our tents. If any of you know anything about this—no matter whose idea it was—I would encourage you to talk to me about it."

With that, she moved along the road, poking through the underbrush, apparently looking for the lost tents. I turned back to Bess and George, who looked as confused as I felt.

"You have got to be kidding me," Bess muttered, shaking her head and walking over to the other side of the road to start looking. "Who would think this is funny?"

Zoe glanced at us, let out a deep sigh, and then followed Bess. "This stinks," I heard her whisper to Bess as the two of them poked through the wildflowers lining the road.

George and I paired up and went back toward the pond, looking around in any shadowy, covered-up spots. We didn't see anything, though—no tents, no sign of footsteps, no trampled grass or broken branches. Dagger came back with us and searched a bit too, but it all felt kind of hopeless.

"This is weird," I whispered to George as we pulled back the fern fronds covering the bank to find—nothing.

George chuckled. "Come on, Detective Drew," she joked. "You're off duty today. Plus, there's probably a totally reasonable explanation. Maybe it was just someone's idea of a practical joke."

"Maybe," I said, remembering that this tour was her dream vacation, and not wanting to step on it. But deep down, my sleuthing senses were tingling.

What had happened to our tents? If this was some kind of prank, I didn't get it. And honestly, none of the people on the tour struck me as big pranksters. Zoe didn't seem to find anything about this trip funny. And while I didn't know him very well, Dagger seemed a little too Zen to pull a tent-stealing gag.

He was standing just a few feet away, and I gave him a friendly smile. "So—this is a little strange, huh?"

Dagger was halfheartedly poking through the plants that covered the pond's bank, and he looked up at me and shrugged. "I didn't expect it," he said, "but it doesn't make much difference. I've slept under the stars before."

Sleeping under the stars. When he put it that way, it didn't sound all that bad. But was it strange that he was so unconcerned that half our gear was missing?

"All right!" Caitlin, who was still out on the road, clapped her hands and shouted. "I think that's it, folks. We need to accept that the tents are gone."

I glanced at George, who nodded, and we walked back through the trees together to rejoin the group that was re-forming on the road. Henry jogged back from where he'd been searching a few yards back, and Bess and Zoe walked back from the other side of the road.

Caitlin glanced around at our faces, still looking a little wary. "Anyone find anything?"

"Yes!" Henry said cheerfully, and when we all turned to him expectantly, pulled a small object out of his pocket.

"I found a four-leaf clover," he said, holding it out for all of us to see. "Good luck, right?"

Caitlin sighed and rolled her eyes. "Great, Henry. That's great. Very funny."

Henry looked offended. "What? We could use all the luck we can get!"

Dagger chuckled, and George smiled too, but Caitlin didn't look amused. She gave Henry a pointed stare, and he shrugged again as the smile faded from his face.

"So what do we do?" Zoe asked, shifting her weight onto one leg and putting her hand on her hip. "Do we go back? I mean, do we really want to keep going if we're not going to have shelter?"

Caitlin didn't have a ready answer. She looked from face to face. "Well," she said finally. "Tents aren't a necessity, really. We could sleep out in the open."

"Under the stars," Dagger put in. "I'm up for that."

There was some murmuring. Bess looked at Zoe and shook her head.

"I don't know," she said slowly. "Nature is beautiful and everything, but I'm not sure I'm up for sleeping out in the open for two nights."

George pursed her lips. "But if we go back, we lose a whole day," she pointed out. "And where would we even get new tents?"

"We'd probably have to stay at the bed-and-breakfast tonight," Caitlin put in, "while Henry and I drove into town to get some new gear. But we would lose a day. Henry and I have a family wedding to go to in three days—we couldn't extend the tour."

George sighed. We all looked around at one another awkwardly.

"Actually, I have an extra tent," Zoe piped up out of nowhere.

"You what?" George said, at the same time Bess gushed, "You do?"

Zoe shrugged. "You can't be too careful."

I tried to catch George's eye—*what?*—but she was still staring at Zoe, who turned to Bess.

"It's a small one, nothing fancy, but there's probably room for one other person, if you want to share with me, Bess."

Bess grinned. "That would be awesome!"

George was shaking her head now, but before she could say anything, Caitlin held up her hand.

"Why don't we take a vote?" she asked. "Who wants to turn back?"

No one raised their hand. I glanced at George; she gave another little shake of her head. *She's wanted to make this trip for months,* I reminded myself. *Of course she's not going to want to cut it short.*

"Okay," Caitlin said, nodding. "Who wants to keep going?"

Dagger, George, and Henry shot up their hands. Zoe glanced at Bess, shrugged, and slowly raised hers. Bess followed suit.

"As long as everyone else is okay sleeping outside, it's fine with me," Bess said quietly.

I realized then that everyone was looking at me, and that I hadn't put up my hand to vote for either choice. *What do I want to do?* I asked myself. Not that it mattered; a clear majority wanted to keep going.

Something about this whole thing still felt very fishy. My sense that something was off—honed by years of sleuthing—was going full force.

But on the other hand, George was giving me the puppy-dog eyes. She has big brown eyes, so her puppy look is pretty effective. And she only pulls out the puppy-dog eyes on very rare occasions. George is by far the most pragmatic of the three of us—she usually goes with the flow. It's pretty rare that her feelings come into play when making decisions.

But now she was clearly having feelings. *Please, please, Nancy, let's keep going, I'm having so much fun* feelings.

I sighed and turned to Caitlin. "Should we be worried?" I asked bluntly. "If our tents were stolen, could that mean someone's following us? Someone with . . . bad intentions?"

George looked disappointed as we all turned to Caitlin.

"I think that's little dramatic," she said, looking away with a casual laugh. "It was probably a prank no one's owning up to, or an innocent mistake. I mean, we're not the only hikers and bikers in this area, and lots of people stop at this picnic spot. My guess is that another group came by, mistook our gear for theirs, and grabbed it."

I wondered if Caitlin's theory sounded as shaky to everyone else as it did to me. *A whole group of hikers came by and none of us heard them?* I wondered. And if it was an innocent mistake, why would they take both our gear and their own?

Then I looked around the circle of faces. Dagger was looking off at the beautiful hills in the distance, seemingly not paying attention. He said he liked sleeping under the stars—maybe he decided to force the issue? Henry was staring down at his hand, picking nervously at a fingernail. I remembered how Caitlin had snapped at him when he'd suggested it might be a prank. *Could it be a brother-sister practical joke we were all caught in the middle of?* I wondered. Maybe that was why Caitlin wanted to keep going.

Finally I sighed and raised my hand. "All right. I vote to keep going."

George grinned and gave a little jump, reaching over to touch my shoulder. "Thanks," she whispered.

We all walked over to where our remaining packs lay, stooping to put our gear back on. My back still ached from the morning's ride.

"I guess it could be sort of nice," I said, catching George's eye. She looked excited. "Sleeping out under the stars."

"Exactly!" George said, smiling again and turning to pick up her bike and throw her leg over the side. "Let's go!"

The ride to the campsite was so beautiful, it pushed the whole mystery of the missing tents out of my mind. Everyone seemed to be in a good mood, laughing and joking. Caitlin noted a mother and baby deer just a few yards away through the trees, and Dagger pointed out another bald eagle flying overhead. With the gorgeous views and the wildlife that seemed to surround us, it was easy to forget our troubles—at least for a little while.

I did notice Bess and Zoe chatting and giggling at the back of the pack like a couple of schoolgirls. At one point I caught George looking at them, a skeptical expression on her face.

"Bess made a new friend," I said cheerily, wondering if George was feeling a tad jealous. Even though she and Bess were about as alike as oil and water, they'd been close their whole lives. But since we'd gotten on the bikes this morning, they'd barely spoken—Bess was too distracted by Zoe.

George just shook her head. "Who brings an extra tent?" she asked, rolling her eyes, then pushed ahead to catch up with Caitlin.

It was a good question. But really, it was just one of many unanswered questions from that morning.

The sun was low in the sky, casting a gorgeous

golden light on the trees, when Caitlin pulled out a map and told us we were just a few minutes from our campsite on the shores of Mystic Lake. We'd seen the lake shimmering in the distance all day, and now I felt a little thrill of accomplishment that we'd actually traveled far enough to reach it. Then my stomach growled, and I realized how hungry I was. It would feel fantastic to get off my bike, relax, and eat dinner.

We passed a curve in the road, and then suddenly the lake appeared before us, glimmering in the late-day sun, which was just starting to dip in the sky to meet the tree line. I gasped appreciatively—it was so peaceful and still, the surface of the water almost looked like a mirror.

"It's beautiful," George said.

Caitlin turned back with a smile. "Wait till you see it in the morning, with a little fog—you'll realize why they named it Mystic Lake."

We pulled our bikes to a stop where a narrow path led into the trees, and then walked them up a gentle slope to a small clearing ringed by Queen Anne's lace and wild daisies. We were on a small hill overlooking the lake. In front of us another path, this one steep and rocky, led down to the shore. On either side, the flowered meadow soon gave way to dark, pine-filled woods.

George laid her bike on the ground and took a deep breath. "This is amazing! It's so pretty here, I'm almost glad we don't have tents to block our view."

Zoe looked up from the ground, where she'd already spread out her pack and was pulling out, in fact, a tiny two-person tent.

"I hope you won't mind one," she said, a sly smile on her lips. "Because a tent is a must for me."

"What led you to bring an extra?" I asked, crinkling my eyebrows in what I hoped looked like a mildly curious expression. Was it just a coincidence that someone stole our tents, and she just happened to pack an extra?

Zoe shrugged. "No offense," she said, looking over at Caitlin, who was laying her pack on the ground, "but I don't trust anyone to prepare as well as I can. I'm always like this when I travel—I bring clean sheets even if we're going to a nice hotel. I bring snacks even if meals are included. It's just this compulsion I have."

A totally weird compulsion. I smiled and nodded, but I wasn't completely convinced by her answer.

Caitlin suggested we take a few minutes to stretch, answer the call of nature if we had to, and start collecting wood for a fire. Zoe and Bess were totally absorbed in setting up their tent, and George had headed into the woods to use the bathroom, so I decided to start looking for firewood.

"Do you think she brought a generator and television, too?" a deep voice asked behind me, startling me so much that I stumbled forward. A strong hand reached out and grabbed my arm, pulling me back to my feet. "Sorry. I didn't mean to startle you."

I turned and found Dagger behind me, a friendly grin on his face.

I shrugged, not wanting to say something about Bess's new friend, but not wanting to make Dagger feel awkward, either. "Different strokes for different folks, I guess."

Dagger nodded. "I suppose I should be happy she

brought the extra tent," he said. "Otherwise we'd prob-ably be at the B and B tonight, and we'd miss all this."

He gestured behind him, at the gorgeous vista of the sun setting over the lake.

"That would have been a shame," I agreed.

For a moment we just took in the beauty of the lake, the quiet calls of birds around us, the wind flow-ing through the trees.

"I don't mean to be unkind toward the young lady," Dagger said. "But this won't be the first time I've slept under the stars, and I'm sure it won't be the last. Look at this amazing view, the food we just ate, the companionship—we should be grateful for what we have."

"I agree," I said quietly. Dagger was framed in the glowing pink light of sunset now, so dark I could barely make out his features.

Then, just as quickly as he'd appeared, he picked up a branch from the ground and was gone.

# CHAPTER THREE

~

# Under the Stars

WITH CAITLIN'S LEADERSHIP, WE BUILT A fire and settled our things around it, then dug out the food for dinner and used the campfire to cook hot dogs, buns, and foil-wrapped baked potatoes. It was a simple meal, but when we were finally ready to eat, it was the most delicious food I'd ever tasted. I let out a groan of happiness when I took my first bite of hot dog.

Henry laughed, shooting me a look of understanding. "Like a gift from heaven," he said with a smile.

"Exactly," I replied.

Caitlin smiled at me. "Part of it is that we don't

realize how many calories we're burning riding our bikes all day. You really work up an appetite."

Zoe took a big bite of her hot dog. "That's one good thing about this tour: I can eat this hot dog and simple carbs with no guilt!"

Bess laughed. "Exercise does have its rewards, Zo!"

Zo? Bess already had a nickname for her new BFF?

"It almost makes up for missing *Revenge* tonight," Zoe went on. "But not quite."

"Omigosh, I love that show."

Bess and Zoe immediately huddled to discuss the last season, throwing out character names and plot twists like they were discussing the trials and travails of their closest friends. I glanced at George next to me; she was staring at Bess's back with a dismayed expression.

"I think we've lost her," I whispered, leaning over to give George's arm a playful squeeze.

"I'm beginning to think we lost her when I asked her to come on this trip," George muttered. "I thought she'd at least try to have fun, but . . ."

"She is having fun," I pointed out, nodding at Bess, who was giggling hysterically at something Zoe had said about catfights.

George frowned. "Maybe I should rephrase that," she said. "I hoped we would have fun together."

Popping the last of his hot dog into his mouth, Henry suddenly stood up and stretched his arms, letting out an exaggerated yawn. "Well," he said, looking around at all of us, "I'm really tired. I suppose it's time to retire to my not-tent."

Dagger chuckled casually, and even Zoe flashed a smile in our direction, but Caitlin's face suddenly went cold.

"Very funny," she said, shooting a glare up at her brother.

Henry smirked. "Come on, Cait," he said. "Don't be a spoilsport just because your first tour isn't up to your usual perfect standards. It doesn't hurt to laugh at yourself once in a while, you know."

But Caitlin's glare didn't lessen. "You can laugh at yourself," she said, her tone turning cold. "In fact, that's all you ever do. But some of us have responsibilities. Some of us need to pay for books for college."

Henry rolled his eyes. "I'm sure Adventures and Company will hire you next summer even if there was a tent snafu on your first trip. Don't worry, you'll still be able to pay for books, sis."

Caitlin was silent for a moment, and I thought she might have calmed down, but then she stood up so suddenly, her paper towel fluttered off her lap to the ground.

"Can I speak to you privately?" she hissed.

Henry looked a little surprised, but nodded. "Um . . . okay," he said, glancing around at the rest of us. "Excuse me."

We all watched silently as Caitlin marched off into the woods, Henry trailing reluctantly behind her.

"She seems a little stressed out," Dagger said, leaning forward to grab a piece of potato and pop it in his mouth. "She should meditate with me tomorrow. You all should."

George asked Dagger about his meditation practices, and soon even Zoe and Bess started taking part in the conversation, Zoe gushing about the Bikram yoga class she was taking. I tried to follow along, but my brain was buzzing with all the strange events of the day. I thought back to the moment when the tents went missing—there seemed to be some tension between Caitlin and Henry then, too. It was clear from the moment that had just passed that Caitlin was pretty upset about the tents going missing, even if she tried to hide it from those of us paying for the tour. What had she said just now? *Some of us need to pay for college?* And Henry had said something about Adventures & Company hiring her anyway?

So maybe this little tour was like a tryout for Caitlin—if it went well, they'd hire her next year?

I tried to remember more about what she'd said when the tents went missing, but my eyes were beginning to droop, and my brain was filling with the fog of exhaustion. I didn't know what time it was, but it had been at least an hour since the sun had dipped below the horizon, and it was dark enough that I couldn't see much just a few yards beyond the fire.

"Right, Nancy?"

George suddenly poked me, and I realized that my eyes had been closed. Had I been sleeping? "What?"

Bess looked at me and giggled, her blue eyes twinkling in the firelight. "Feeling a little tired, huh?"

I shook my head. "I guess so. We did do a lot of biking today."

George nodded. "Well, I was talking about my favorite part of our ride today, but maybe we should turn in instead. I have to admit, I'm pretty worn out too."

Zoe nodded and stretched, yawning the same kind of exaggerated yawn Henry had faked earlier—except hers seemed real. "Yeah, let's say good night," she agreed. "Our cozy tent beckons."

Bess glanced at George and me uncomfortably, like she was feeling a little bad about the tent situation. But I shook my head at her.

"And my cozy sleeping bag beckons," I said. "Honestly, I'm so tired tonight, I don't think it matters whether I'm in a tent or not. I'm going to be out cold as soon as I'm horizontal."

Bess smiled, looking a little relieved.

We all stood—Dagger, too—and Bess and Zoe walked over to their tent on the outskirts of the clearing, while George and I grabbed our sleeping bags to set them up just outside the fire circle. Dagger said good night to all of us, took his sleeping bag, and started walking down the rocky slope to the lake.

"I saw a little flat area down here to set up my sleeping bag on," he said, when he turned and saw me watching him curiously. "I love the sound of water lapping the shore."

That sounded nice. I nodded. "See you in the morning, Dagger. Sleep well."

As George and I went to leave the fire circle, a figure suddenly came bursting out of the darkness—Henry!

"Hey!" he said, looking around at the empty fire circle. "Everyone going to bed?"

George nodded apologetically. "We're pretty tired," she admitted. "You and Caitlin have been gone awhile. What happened to her?"

Henry's face started to tense, then stopped abruptly, like he suddenly thought better of it. He made his face neutral. "Oh, she went to bed," he said. "Said she was feeling tired. Our sleeping bags are set up in the meadow, right over there." He pointed only several yards away, but it was so dark that I couldn't see much of anything beyond his fingertip.

"Okay," said George, nodding awkwardly. "Well, good night."

Henry smiled. "Sleep tight," he said, walking over to the fire and starting to push some rocks over what remained of the embers. "Hope the mosquitoes don't bite."

As I shot George an alarmed look, Henry turned back around with another smirk. "Just kidding," he added. "The mosquitoes made such a buffet out of my legs, they must be full by now. Unlike the bears."

George shook her head. "Such a joker," she muttered, picking up her sleeping bag and stepping over one of the big logs that circled the fire pit. "Ha-ha."

I followed George sleepily about fifty feet away

from the fire pit, then did as she did, spreading my bag on the ground. We went together to use the makeshift bathroom Caitlin had dug out near an old oak tree in the woods, then came back and settled into our nice, cozy sacks. The air had gotten a little cool, and the flannelly warmth felt really good.

I settled my head on the pillow and closed my eyes, breathing in deeply. "The air smells nice," I said. "Kind of misty and piney."

"I know," George agreed. "Tents or no, I'm really enjoying this trip."

"It just got a little breezier," I said, turning over onto my side and hugging my pillow. "It feels good."

I settled into my favorite sleeping position, letting my jaw drop open on the pillow, and felt that delicious *I am in the perfect position, about to drift off* feeling spread over my body.

That was when the first drop hit me on the shoulder.

I blinked my eyes open, surprised, just in time to see the sky open up as it started to pour.

# CHAPTER FOUR

❧

# Too Close for Comfort

I SHOT UP INTO A SITTING POSITION. Rain poured down onto my hair and dripped into my eyes, and the driving streams and the dark made it hard to see George's face just a few feet away.

When I finally could see her, she didn't look happy.

"Son of a biscuit!" she hissed.

At that moment several things happened at once. I heard Caitlin let out a little yelp, presumably as she woke up and took in what had happened. I saw Henry run over from where he'd been lingering at the fire pit, I guessed to help his sister. And then, after a moment, a small but blinding beam of light hit me right in the face. I squinted, trying to see where it was coming from, and saw that a dark figure was shooting a flashlight out the front flap of Zoe's tent.

"Guys, come in here!"

It was Bess's voice.

I squirmed out of my already-soaked sleeping bag and looked at George.

"What are you waiting for?" she asked, already on her feet and shoving her folded-up bag under her arm. "Let's get in there!"

I pulled my sleeping bag off my feet and balled it up into something small enough to carry, then sprang up and darted across the meadow toward the flashlight beam. I pushed into the narrow fabric entrance, and I immediately felt the slick, squishy feeling of a sleeping bag beneath me, followed by a yelp from Zoe: "Hey, watch it!"

George pushed in right behind me, knocking me off my feet and sending me sprawling over Zoe's head.

"Arrgh!" she whined. "Guys! It's pretty tight in here."

Bess had pulled the flashlight back inside, and now she aimed it at the wall so we could all see one another in the ambient light. Whoa! Zoe was right— the tent was teeny, a little tight for two people, really. For the four of us (and our sleeping bags) to fit in there, we were going to have to sleep practically on top of one another.

I pulled myself back into a crouch and crept over Zoe, trying to settle myself in a little pocket of empty space by the door. "Sorry, guys."

"Don't be sorry," said Bess, but I heard Zoe sigh loudly. "We couldn't leave you out there to get soaked," Bess went on. "This is, like, the worst bike tour ever! Did you guys see Caitlin and Henry?"

"No, but I heard her yell." Like me, George was clearly struggling to find space in the tiny shelter, and now she swung her rear end around and settled it on Bess's sleeping bag. Bess wordlessly scooched back to make room. "I'm sure they're used to bad weather, but I don't think anyone's very happy about this shower."

Bess glanced at Zoe and bit her lip. "They'll just

be stuck out there getting soaked. Should we invite them in?"

Zoe widened her eyes. "Are you kidding? I didn't bring an extra tent to try to fit everyone in. Where would we sleep?"

Bess shrugged, looking frustrated. "We wouldn't all fit in here to sleep. But maybe they could at least get out of the rain."

Zoe shook her head forcefully, and George sighed.

"Never mind," she said, moving toward the entrance. "I'll check on them."

Before any of us could stop her, George was outside the tent, running through the rain. "Caitlin? Henry?" I heard her calling. "Dagger?"

Silence fell in the tent, and I looked awkwardly from Bess to Zoe. "I hope they're okay," I said.

"I'm sure they are," Zoe said quietly, the annoyed edge fading from her voice. "They're the gung-ho nature people, remember? And it's just rain, after all. They'll dry."

Bess and I were quiet for another minute, neither of

us sure what to say, when George pushed her way back into the tent.

"They say they're fine," she said. "Caitlin and Henry are trying to rig up a tarp she brought to block the rain. And Dagger says he likes it—it makes him feel 'closer to nature' or something." She shrugged, sitting back down on Bess's sleeping bag and running a hand through her soaking-wet hair.

Bess squealed. "Hey, watch it!" she said. "I invited you guys in here to keep you dry, not to make me wet."

"See?" Zoe asked, turning to Bess and me with a satisfied smile. "All the people left out there are the dedicated nature people. It won't hurt them to get a little wet."

George looked at her and frowned. "I think you can enjoy nature and still not want to get wet."

Zoe rolled her eyes. "I guess," she said, and sighed. "Listen, your sleeping bags are soaking wet. Can you throw them outside to make more room?"

George's frown deepened. "And where will Nancy and I sleep?"

Zoe shrugged, as though the answer didn't matter very much to her, but Bess spoke up before she could reply. "Maybe Zoe and I could climb out of our sleeping bags and unzip them," she suggested. "We could sleep on top of one and share the other like a blanket."

Zoe looked distinctly unexcited about this idea, but George spoke before she could say anything. "Great. Let's do it."

Bess jumped into action, and Zoe hesitated only a moment before wriggling out of her sleeping bag too. It took some maneuvering, but soon we had Bess's sleeping bag unzipped and spread out on the tent floor. We all got on it, trying to negotiate a way for all four of us to sleep in the small space without being on top of one another. In the end, we ended up sleeping side by side, all lined up like railroad tracks.

We were so close that when I tried to snuggle into the sleeping bag beneath me, Zoe yelped in alarm.

"Ouch! You just kneed me in the butt."

"Sorry," I murmured, trying to get comfortable in the position I was in. It was tough—I felt all stretched out and unnatural. For a second, I thought longingly of that moment just before the rain had fallen when I'd been about to fall asleep out in the cool, misty air.

That would have been nice.

Bess groaned. "Cuz, stop shaking your leg, please."

George stopped abruptly. We were close enough that we could all feel it. "Sorry," she said. "I'm a little uncomfortable."

Zoe snorted. "You're uncomfortable?" she asked. "Because I was a lot more comfortable before you guys showed up. No offense."

George sat up, and even in the darkness I could see her eyes shooting daggers at Zoe. "No offense?" she asked. "Gee, Zoe, I was a lot more comfortable before we came in here too. No offense."

Uh-oh. "Guys," I began, trying to use my most diplomatic tone. "We're in kind of tight quarters here, so . . ."

Now Zoe sat up too. "Why don't you go back out there?" she asked, pointing to the closed door of the tent, outside which the rain poured down with a constant *rat-a-tat-a-tat*. "After all, you voted to keep going even knowing we had no tents, right? I mean, it must have occurred to you that it might rain?"

George set her jaw. "It did," she said, "but I thought the risk was worth it to enjoy the trip I'd been dreaming about for months."

Zoe groaned. "You outdoorsy people," she said with a sigh. "All about experiencing nature, until it gets a little uncomfortable, and then you're just like us."

"Us who?" George asked.

Zoe smirked. "Us, like me and Bess," she said, looking back at Bess, who was on my other side. "The reasonable people, who like shelter and good sheets and bring extra tents to save your butts."

Even in the dark, I could tell George was more than miffed at that, but Bess just giggled. "Can we just go to sleep, guys?" she asked. "The sooner we go to sleep, the sooner we wake up in the morning, and the sooner this whole experience is over."

"Amen to that," Zoe agreed, and settled back down on her pillow.

Everything was silent for a moment. I hoped, desperately, that the conversation was over and we could all go to sleep. I closed my eyes.

But George wasn't finished yet.

"Gee, cuz," she said after a moment, a chill creeping into her voice. "I'm so sorry that my dream trip has been such a nightmare for you."

Bess was silent for a moment, then let out an awkward laugh. "Come on," she said. "You don't agree that this trip has been kind of a bust so far?"

"I've seen some amazing scenery and met some really cool people," George said. "I've seen more wildlife in one day than I've ever seen before!"

Zoe snorted. "And I've noticed that someone stole our tents two hours in, and things have just gone downhill from there!" she cried. "Come on, George. You haven't noticed that our leaders don't seem to agree on anything? And that Dagger is a total weirdo? And that we got a total downpour tonight and we're all packed in here like sardines?"

"Yeah," Bess added quietly, before George could

respond. "This hasn't exactly been my dream vacation, cuz."

George was quiet for a few seconds. When she spoke, her voice was full of barely restrained anger. "I'm so sorry I inconvenienced you by wanting to share my trip with you," she said sarcastically. "I thought it wouldn't be a big deal for you to go outside your comfort zone for three days, to celebrate my birthday."

Bess didn't move, but when she spoke, her voice was angry too. "I came for you, cuz," she said. "But this isn't my thing. You can't make me like it."

"I only came for my friend too—for Gemma," Zoe said with a sigh. "Stupid mono."

George lay back down on her pillow. Again, I hoped the conversation was over, but George fired one parting shot:

"Bess, for your thirteenth birthday, I went to a 'makeover slumber party' for you. You decided I would look better blond, and we snuck out to the drugstore, and I let you bleach my hair—remember? It was orange for a week."

Bess hesitated a second before responding. "I remember."

"But I never complained," George went on. "That party was, like, the best night of your life. And that made me happy. Because cousins make sacrifices to make each other happy."

With that, George flopped onto her side.

Bess didn't say anything else, and for several minutes there was silence in the tent. The rain *pat-pat-pat*ting on the roof was the only sound.

I stretched my legs again, struggling to get comfortable, wishing I could recapture the cozy warmth I'd felt before the rain began. But that didn't seem terribly likely. The tension in the tent was thick enough to cut with a knife, and I wondered if I'd ever get to sleep now.

But in the end my exhaustion won out. Maybe twenty minutes after George said her last words, I finally drifted off to sleep.

I awoke hours later, still in the dark, to a scream.

# CHAPTER FIVE

### ❧

# Gone

I SHOT UPRIGHT. IT WAS DARK STILL, BUT there was an edge of pale light creeping in, like dawn wasn't far off. The rain had stopped, and there was total silence outside our tent. It was just light enough to make out Bess, George, and Zoe next to me, all still sleeping peacefully.

Had I dreamed it? I bit my lip, wondering if I'd really heard what I'd thought. Maybe it was just the tail end of a nightmare? Maybe . . .

But then I heard something scuffling past our tent. Someone was awake out there.

I scooted from beneath Bess's sleeping-bag blanket and crept out of the tent. I stood up in the little meadow, looking around. It seemed darker outside than it had inside the tent, and it took a minute for my eyes to adjust. I looked to the right, down over the lake, then straight ahead, then to my left. . . .

"Auugh!"

Panic seized at my lungs. Dagger was standing there, no more than five feet in front of me, silently watching.

"Sorry if I startled you," he said after a moment in his calm, unruffled voice. "What are you doing up?"

I swallowed. Should I tell him? Let's face it: Either Dagger would be nice and help me figure out where the scream came from, or he had caused the scream, and letting him know I'd heard it would end badly for me.

"I . . . what are you doing up?" I said finally.

Dagger smiled. "I was just about to start my predawn meditation," he said, gesturing behind him, where I could now make out a bright-blue blanket and a little dish of incense. "Sunrise isn't far off, and it promises to be breathtaking. Would you like to join me?"

"Ah . . . no, thanks," I said, scanning the clearing as I remembered my real purpose in coming out here. Had someone really screamed? Was a member of our group in trouble? "Um, the truth is, Dagger, I woke up because I could have sworn I heard somebody scream."

Dagger frowned. "Ah. Yes, I heard something too, a minute or so before you came out. I thought it was just a large bird. Nature can be a bit noisy before dawn."

I kept looking around the clearing. There was no sign of Caitlin or Henry, but hadn't they relocated after the rain began? Maybe they were in the woods, safe under their tarp, fast asleep. A prickle of guilt entered my thoughts at the memory that we'd slept safe and dry in a tent, while they'd had to struggle in the harsh weather.

"I think I'm going to check on Caitlin and Henry," I said finally, turning to Dagger with a little shrug. "Just to be sure they're okay. Do you know where they moved when the rain started?"

Dagger pushed his lips to the side. Was he thinking, or was he uncomfortable with what I'd said? "I wouldn't check on them," he said after a few seconds. "The truth is, I wanted to preserve their privacy, but I heard them having a fairly serious argument not long before the birdcall. That's what woke me up—though it was nicely timed to prepare me for my sunrise meditation." He smiled briefly, then turned serious. "It sounded . . . unpleasant. You know how fraught sibling relationships can be."

Huh. I didn't know, actually, because I didn't have brothers or sisters. Even so, Dagger's information made me want to check on Caitlin and Henry more, not less.

"What were they arguing about?" I asked.

"I couldn't make everything out, but it seemed to center on a text message, of all things," Dagger said. "Henry got a text message that seemed to cause Caitlin some concern. I heard something along the lines of 'I can't believe you're involved in this,' followed by 'It's none of your business.' It was very heated for a few minutes. Then there was silence."

*I can't believe you're involved in this.* Those words made me nervous. But even so, something seemed weird about Dagger's story, and it took me a minute to figure out what it was.

*A text message, of all things.* That was it! As the website had warned us, the Mystic Lake area seemed to offer no cell service whatsoever. George's, Bess's, and my phones hadn't worked at all since that morning. It gave me kind of a creepy feeling, honestly—just realizing how cut off we were, and how much I normally depended on my smartphone.

So was Dagger lying about the fight?

Was he trying to distract me from figuring out who had screamed?

"I'm going to check on them," I blurted quickly, and ran off toward the edge of the woods before Dagger could stop me.

"CAITLIN! HENRY?" I ran into the trees, poking around the edge of the forest where I figured Henry and Caitlin would have set up their tarp if they were in a hurry. Plenty of trees grew close enough together to string a tarp between; there was no need to delve deeper into the woods.

I could hear Dagger running after me. Though I wasn't sure whether he was a threat, this made me run faster. "CAITLIN! HENRY!" I ran around the edge of the meadow, peering into the still-dark woods. Dagger's footsteps were just a few yards behind me now. He was closing the distance between us, not saying a word.

"Hey, what's going on?"

Bess's voice cut through the predawn silence, and both Dagger and I turned to see her standing outside the tent, squinting in our direction.

"I thought I heard a scream," I called. Dagger seemed to go limp, his arms falling flatly by his side.

"Yes, we're looking for Caitlin and Henry, to check on them," he said. "Nancy, I believe their new campsite is over there."

He pointed farther down to our left. Was he only helping because Bess saw him? I pushed the thought out of my mind; I wasn't going to try figure that out now, and I was still worried about Caitlin and Henry.

Sure enough, when I ran in the direction Dagger had pointed, I could just see a bright-blue tarp strung between two trees, with what looked like sleeping bags set underneath.

"Caitlin! Henry! Is everything all right?" I called, running closer.

But when I was still a few yards away, I could see that both sleeping bags were empty—balled up and tossed aside, as if their inhabitants had taken off quickly.

A chill ran up my spine. Maybe one of them had gotten up to use the bathroom, but both of them? Why would they both be missing from their beds before dawn?

"CAITLIN! HENRY!"

Dagger's footsteps came to a sudden halt behind me. "Oh no. Where could they be?" he asked in his perpetually calm voice.

Bess ran into the woods behind us, followed closely by George. "What's going on?" George demanded.

It was Dagger who filled her in this time: "Caitlin and Henry aren't in their sleeping bags. Nancy thinks she heard a scream."

George widened her eyes in alarm. Bess pressed her hand to her mouth.

"We need to find them," I said unnecessarily.

George nodded. "I'll check out the bathroom spot. Let's all split up and look around. Okay?"

"Okay," I agreed quickly, glad not to be alone anymore—or alone with Dagger, really.

We split up and ran around the edge of the woods, calling for them. Bess ran back toward the road to see if they might have gone out there. George quickly ran back from the makeshift bathroom to report that no one was there—no one was anywhere nearby.

"I don't see any sign of them," she whispered to me, while Dagger searched the rocky area leading to the lake. "They're gone! It's just like the tents."

I felt my stomach flip. What was going on here? It didn't make sense for several tents to disappear into the wilderness with no sign; it definitely didn't make sense for two teenagers to do so, when they were supposed to be leading a tour.

*Where are you, Caitlin and Henry?*

We all kept looking; searching farther and farther from the campsite, going deeper into the woods. The sun was beginning to rise now and, as Dagger had promised, was creating quite a gorgeous display over the lake. But we were all too tense to appreciate it. Nobody was meditating.

I sighed and stopped for a moment in the clearing. My heart was pounding, both from the exertion of running around nonstop and from the creeping feeling that something terrible had happened. I looked at Bess, who was searching the grass for clues—dropped items, footprints, anything.

"I'm going to go back to the tent and wake up Zoe," I said.

Bess nodded. "Yeah, I think it's time."

I started walking toward the tent, the tall grass sliding against my bare legs. I paused, just briefly, to turn to my left and take in the bright pink-and-purple sunrise glimmering over the lake. George was right: This area was beautiful. *Shame it seems so dangerous,* I thought.

Then a figure suddenly came at me from the woods, and my heart stopped.

"Zoe!" I cried.

She blinked at me curiously, then pushed her curly dark hair behind one ear. Her face was still creased from the lacy sleep mask she wore. "Hey, Nancy. What's up?"

"Where were you?" I demanded, looking somewhat accusatorily behind her to the path she'd taken from the woods.

Zoe pouted. "Um, I woke up and had to pee, so I went in the woods?" she said. "It's traumatic enough without you acting like it's a major felony, you know."

"You didn't hear us all running around yelling for Caitlin and Henry for half an hour?" I pressed on. *You didn't even care that the three of us were missing from the tent before dawn?* my inner voice continued. I knew Zoe seemed a little selfish sometimes, but really?

Zoe rubbed her eyes and sighed. "Since you mention it, yes, I woke up just a few minutes ago and did notice that you and Bess and George seemed to be playing some kind of hide-and-seek thing out here," she said, sounding annoyed. "But I really had to go. So I figured I'd take care of business first."

I shook my head. I still wasn't sure whether Zoe's behavior was shady or we just had completely opposite personalities. And either way, this wasn't getting us any closer to finding Caitlin or Henry.

"Our leaders are missing," I said curtly. "Both of them. I heard a scream about half an hour ago. Can you help us look, please?"

Zoe raised her eyebrows. "Caitlin and Henry are missing?" she asked. "Are you serious?"

"Can you look?" I asked, nodding.

Zoe let out an amazed sigh. "Uh, yeah," she said, turning back toward the woods. "CAITLIN! HENR— oh my gosh!"

I was headed to the tent, but I turned to see what had Zoe so rattled. Some kind of wildlife? Broken nail?

But when I saw what she was yelling about, I let out a little yelp too. "Oh no!"

Because Henry was staggering out of the woods, covered in blood.

# CHAPTER SIX

~

# More Bad News

HENRY WAS MOANING. HE STUMBLED OUT of the trees into the tall grass and collapsed into a heap.

"Henry, are you okay?" Zoe was asking, running over to his side as I was running from the tent.

"You're bleeding!" I cried.

Henry moaned again and rubbed his eyes. "No, I'm fine. Physically, I'm fine."

"What happened to Caitlin?" I asked urgently.

Henry moaned again, then closed his eyes. "She's gone," he said simply.

"Gone?" Zoe asked, as I repeated, "Gone?"

"Where is she?" Zoe continued.

Bess came running up from the meadow. "Henry, thank goodness!"

I could see George coming out from the woods on the other side of the meadow, and Dagger's head peeping over the edge of the rocky slope that led to the lake. They must have heard the commotion too.

Henry sat up, running his hand through his hair. "I don't know where she is," he said, quietly enough that I had to lean in to hear. "I woke up, and her sleeping bag was empty. Then I heard a scream."

So I did hear a scream. "So you went after her?" I asked.

Henry nodded, his face drawn. "I went in what I thought was the direction of the scream, but I couldn't find her. Then I thought maybe I'd heard wrong, maybe she'd just gotten up to use the bathroom, but she wasn't there, either. I've spent the last half hour or so running all through the woods, looking for her."

Zoe gestured to the blood on his arms, legs, and face. "You're bleeding, Henry. Why?"

Henry looked down at himself, surprised. "Wow," he said breathlessly. "Honestly, I've been so freaked, I was just crashing around through bushes and stuff. I guess I scratched myself up pretty bad. And I must have touched my arms or legs, then touched my face."

George walked toward him and took off her sweatshirt, dabbing at his face with the sleeve. Sure enough, all the blood wiped off.

"You're right," she said. "You have some scratches, and you must have moved the blood around with your hands."

I tapped my lip, thinking. It was a relief that Henry hadn't been attacked, or anything that serious. But I was still really worried about what had happened to Caitlin. Where could she have gone?

"Henry, can you think of anything Caitlin might be doing?" I asked. "Does she often stalk off after arguments? Dagger said he overheard you fighting."

Henry frowned. "Fighting? We weren't fighting." He shot Dagger a look, and I couldn't figure out whether it was confused or challenging.

Dagger shrugged, his Zen calm still evident on his face. "I overheard a heated discussion, maybe. About a text message?"

Henry's face reddened. "Text message? What are you talking about, man? No one gets service out here."

Dagger shrugged again. "I am only relaying what I heard."

Henry scowled. "You heard wrong, dude." He rubbed his nose and sighed. "Caitlin and I pick on each other all the time—just like all brothers and sisters do. But like I said, I woke up to find her missing. There was no fight."

Huh. "So you have no idea why she might have run off, or what she might be doing?" I asked.

Henry looked up at me, surprised. "No," he said emphatically. "Listen, this is really unlike her. She's the one who lectures me about the dangers of going on hikes alone. And she gets tense, sure, but she's not the kind to have some kind of tantrum and stalk off."

In the silence that followed Henry's words, the six of us looked at one another. I could read from everyone's expressions that we were all at a loss. Finally I asked the question I sensed we were all asking ourselves:

"What do we do now?"

We decided to move to the fire pit to have a serious conversation.

"I hate to say it," Dagger said, speaking first, "but it seems that Caitlin may be well and truly missing. Gone, as Henry said. We've all been looking for her for at least an hour now, with no response."

George nodded. "I think it's time to call someone," she said, looking earnestly at Henry.

But Henry looked confused. "Call someone?" he asked. "Um, my cell doesn't work out here. I don't know about you guys."

"Caitlin told us she had a satellite phone to use in emergencies," I spoke up. "In case anybody got hurt, or needed medical attention. Or went missing." Why didn't he know this?

Henry still looked mystified. "She said that?"

Bess frowned at him. "Yeah. You were right there, actually."

Henry's face reddened. "Oh, well . . . I mean . . . Caitlin took care of all the logistical stuff on this trip," he said. "But okay, if we have a phone, totally, we should call someone now."

He stood up from the log he was sitting on, and I took the opportunity to scan the circle. If Caitlin's disappearance involved foul play—if anyone from our tour was involved in whatever had happened to her—then presumably, calling the authorities would make them uncomfortable. Under the circumstances, it seemed unlikely that anyone would jump up and scream for Henry to stop, but people wear their discomfort in telling ways—they fidget, break eye contact, remove themselves from the conversation. When I looked around, though, nobody was doing anything I would immediately associate with being uncomfortable. Dagger was scratching his cheek, watching the scene intently. Zoe had her arms crossed and looked slightly bored and annoyed—the same expression she'd worn for most of the trip. Bess and George, of course, looked as bewildered by this morning's events as I felt.

We all got up slowly and followed Henry over to where he and Caitlin had slept under the tarp, and where they'd placed their packs. Looking a little uneasy, Henry walked over to Caitlin's backpack and gingerly unzipped it. As we watched, he began searching the main compartment, then the front pocket, the side pocket, a rear pocket. . . .

"You have no idea where she might have kept it?" George asked.

Henry looked up, wearing a frustrated expression. "I told you, Caitlin knew all the logistical stuff for these tours," he said.

"And what *do* you know?" Bess asked pointedly. "What are you usually in charge of?"

Henry looked uneasy again. He didn't answer, just looked back into the pack and rooted around some more. "It's not here. Maybe she put it in the cooler bag with the food."

We all waited while Henry trooped us back to the

fire pit, where the cooler had been kept. He walked over to where it had been set the night before . . . and frowned. Then he looked around the fire pit, then back at the same spot, then at us.

"You don't know where the food is?" Zoe asked incredulously.

Henry shook his head. "It's not that," he said. "It's that I think the food's been . . . taken."

# CHAPTER SEVEN

# Time to Get Help

"STOLEN?" I ASKED. WAS HE SERIOUS? FIRST the tents, then Caitlin, then the food?

Henry nodded. "I know we left it here last night. And now . . ." He gestured at the empty spot.

Dagger moved forward, looking down where Henry had been searching and then scanning the whole fire pit, as Henry had. "Is there any chance Caitlin moved the food because of the rain?" He had a point. Knowing how sensible Caitlin was, she'd probably stashed it under a rock or something to keep it from getting soaked.

Henry shook his head. "I seriously doubt it. We were scrambling around like chickens with our heads cut off trying to get that tarp up. I don't know when she would have had a chance to move the food."

"So just to clarify," I said, "we're without food and without the emergency phone. Right?"

Henry looked at me for a moment, then nodded. "We can keep looking for a bit," he said, "but it seems that way, yeah."

Bess sighed. "So now we really have to ask ourselves: What do we do now?"

Henry looked pained. "I . . . what do you guys think?"

"We should contact the police," I said, "one way or another. Caitlin's been missing for about an hour now, by your timeline, Henry. And now it looks like someone's stolen our food, and our emergency phone is gone," I added. "It seems like . . . someone is out to sabotage this trip."

At my words, I could see everyone shudder a little bit. I'm sure the thought had occurred to all of us, but saying it out loud made it seem truer somehow.

Henry sighed. "I just hate to leave Caitlin," he said. "On the off chance she did get mad about something and wander off and get hurt, or something like that."

"I thought you said you didn't fight," George pointed out.

"We didn't," Henry said, "but you know how girls are."

When his comment was greeted with stony silence, Henry looked up and seemed to recognize that he was talking to four girls, and only one guy.

"I mean . . . ," he said. "Uh . . ."

"If we left, where would we go?" Zoe asked in a crisp voice. "Do you even know how to get to the police?"

Henry nodded. "I mean, I'm not totally useless," he said, with a crooked smile nobody smiled back at. He dug into the pocket of his shorts and pulled out a crumpled paper. "I have a map of our ride, and the area," he said, unfolding it. "According to this, there's a ranger station about"—he squinted at the map and frowned—"two hours' ride from here? Give or take a few minutes."

He passed the map to Dagger, who was standing closest, and Dagger spread it out on the ground so we could all look. The map looked incredibly confusing to me, but Henry pointed out the ranger station, and it didn't look impossibly far.

"I think we should go," Zoe said, crossing her arms again and hugging herself. "If nothing else, we'll be safe with the police."

She didn't say more, but she didn't have to. Her meaning was clear. *We're not safe out here.*

Henry looked sincerely pained. "I agree. I just . . ."

Dagger looked at him, raising his eyebrows. "If we leave, we could be leaving Caitlin?" he asked.

Henry nodded, looking grateful. "Exactly."

Dagger nodded sagely. Then he looked around at the rest of us and raised his hand. "I propose that we stay here at the campsite for one hour more. We can gather our things, try to find something to eat. If, in one hour's time, Caitlin hasn't returned, we'll leave for the ranger station. Okay?"

We all looked around at one another, nodding.

"Okay," I said, and was soon echoed by Henry, George, Bess, and Zoe.

Once we'd decided, Henry went back to the woods to pack up his and Caitlin's gear, and Zoe and Bess took off to start breaking down the tent. Zoe quickly rebuffed my and George's offers to help.

"No offense," she said, "but it's a small tent, and I think this is a 'too many cooks' kind of thing."

After Bess and Zoe departed, Dagger went back over to collect his meditation supplies and move them down to the little plateau he'd slept on by the lake. "This seems like a perfect time to clear my mind and connect with the universe," he explained to us. "Care to join me?"

George and I looked at each other blankly, then shook our heads.

"You have fun," said George. Satisfied, Dagger disappeared down the rocky slope.

"I think it would take bleach and about three days of scrubbing to clear my mind this morning," George muttered when he was out of earshot.

I shivered. "Do you think we're in danger?" I asked.

"I don't know."

I paused, then put voice to the question that had been bumping around in my mind all day—the one I wanted most to ignore. "Do you think someone on the tour is behind all this?"

George was silent for a moment. I could feel her shiver too. "I don't know," she said, more softly.

For a few minutes we were quiet, just watching the lake, which was still sparkling gorgeously in the sun, like it didn't realize that a girl was missing and our tents and food were gone and we were hours away from getting any help.

I heard George sigh, and put a hand on her arm. "I'm sorry your birthday trip has gone so wrong," I said.

She shook her head. "Thanks. But I'm not worried about that. I just want Caitlin to be safe," she said.

I nodded. At that moment Bess's giggle rang out from the meadow, where she and Zoe were struggling to fold the tent small enough to fit back into Zoe's pack. George looked over in her cousin's direction, and all at once I remembered their argument the night before.

"Maybe you should talk to Bess," I suggested. "Try to work it out?"

George shook her head. "Why bother?" she muttered. "I'm still kind of mad at her for complaining so much. Besides," she added, nodding in Henry's direction, "we have bigger problems to worry about."

# CHAPTER EIGHT

# Bad to Worse

AN HOUR LATER, MY STOMACH WAS RUMBLING.
Dagger had helped us collect a "breakfast" of edible
greens and berries from the forest, and we'd split a
couple of protein bars from Zoe's "snack stash," plus
the bars George's parents had packed for us, but I was
still ravenous from our long ride the day before.

There was no sign of Caitlin.

"We should go," Dagger said finally, gently, once
we'd finished eating.

Henry nodded, balling a protein bar wrapper up in
his hand. "Okay."

We all dragged our gear over to where the bikes waited, near the side of the road.

We picked up our bikes and climbed on—all except, I quickly realized, Zoe. She held her bike upright but was staring back at the campsite. When I shifted to get a look at her face, I realized she looked stricken.

"Zoe?" I asked. "Are you okay?"

She shook her head, not taking her eyes off the woods. "Are you . . . are you sure it's a good idea to leave?" she asked. "Maybe we should just wait a little longer."

Surprised, I looked at Bess.

"We talked about this, Zo," she said gently. "It's best for us to get help. Come on, she'll be okay."

Zoe shook her head again, looking down at her feet. When she looked back up, I realized there was a tear trickling down her cheek. She was crying.

"I just can't stand the thought that she might be hurt or . . . or . . ." She swiped at her eyes, shooting me a challenging look. "We don't know what happened to her. She might need us."

I leaned over to touch her arm. "Zoe," I said softly. "She needs help right now. Help from the authorities. Come on, we all agreed on that."

Zoe seemed to pull herself together, then finally nodded.

"Sorry I'm being such a drama queen. You're right. It's just . . ."

"I know," I said quietly, wondering why Zoe was suddenly so teary. "It doesn't feel right, but it is."

Henry, who looked utterly bewildered by this whole display, nodded. Everyone lined up in formation, ready to take off. But I lingered back beside Zoe.

"Zoe," I whispered, "is there a reason you're so worried? You don't . . . know anything we don't, do you?"

Zoe didn't meet my eye. She was climbing on her bike, and she looked down at the ground as she settled on the seat and put one foot on the pedal.

"No," she said finally, shaking her head.

I nodded and adjusted my bike helmet. But I couldn't resist one glance back at her before we took off.

She was glaring right at Dagger, her expression unreadable.

It was a quiet ride through the woods. Henry had told us that we'd be riding along this road for ten miles, at which point we'd cross a river and turn off onto a smaller path. Nobody seemed able to think of much to say. Even the normally chatty Bess and Zoe were quiet, each staring ahead, thinking their separate thoughts.

As we were riding, something occurred to me, and I noticed that Dagger had fallen to the back of the pack, a few bike lengths behind the others. I slowed my pedaling to fall beside him.

"Hi," I said, giving him a friendly smile.

"Hello," he said with a nod. "How are you holding up?"

"I'm okay," I said with a shrug. "Can I ask you a question, though? Something's bothering me."

Dagger nodded. "Perhaps it's the same thing that's bothering me," he suggested.

"Perhaps," I agreed. "Well . . . you said you heard

Henry and Caitlin having a pretty bad argument before she disappeared. But Henry says they didn't fight at all."

Dagger nodded grimly. "Yes. I find that troubling," he said.

"This may sound silly, but are you sure you heard them fighting?" I asked. "You weren't just . . . dreaming or something like that?"

Dagger shook his head. "I heard an argument, clear as day. And there was a lot of emotion involved," he added. "Caitlin, at least, sounded very upset. I can't imagine why Henry is denying it. But then, I don't understand many things about Henry."

*Like how he doesn't seem to know anything about this trip,* I filled in. But that was more understandable, if Henry was used to Caitlin taking charge. Could any sane person really have a fight with their sister and not realize it was a fight?

Or was Henry—more likely—just trying to hide something?

I hadn't forgotten that Dagger had acted slightly

weird this morning too. He'd claimed to think the scream was a birdcall and had discouraged me from checking on Henry and Caitlin. I still shuddered when I remembered his footsteps behind me as I ran toward their campsite, and the way he'd stopped short when Bess had come out of the tent and called to me.

Was he about to hurt me? Stop me from going after Caitlin?

As much as I hated to believe it, I knew it was possible that someone in the group had something to do with Caitlin's disappearance. And the most likely suspects were Henry—who'd been missing, at first, with her—and Dagger, who'd also been up when I got out of our tent.

Dagger said he'd overheard a fight. Henry said it never happened.

Who was lying?

"Excuse me." I suddenly realized that Dagger was snapping his fingers, trying to get my attention. Oops. I'd wandered off into sleuthyville there.

"Yes?" I smiled, trying to look like someone who

wasn't suspecting him of kidnapping and potentially murder.

Dagger raised his eyebrows. "Shouldn't we have passed the river by now?"

Huh. I thought about it, and soon realized Dagger was right. We'd been riding for at least an hour. Surely we'd gone ten miles?

"I think you're right," I told Dagger.

Dagger pedaled faster to get closer to Henry, calling for him. When he had the coleader's attention, he insisted that we stop. Henry obeyed, and we all pulled over to the side of the road. Dagger moved up to confront Henry, stepping off his bike and frowning at him.

"Where is the map?"

Henry looked confused. "Hold on, hold on. Why are we stopping?"

"Give me the map," Dagger insisted.

Henry frowned at him. "Not until you tell me what's going on, man. What's got your nose out of joint?"

Dagger let out an exasperated sigh as the rest of us got off our bikes and gathered closer. "You said we would ride ten miles and pass a river. We have not passed a river. And we've surely gone more than ten miles, haven't we?"

Henry looked thoughtful. "Huh. I guess . . ."

Dagger held out his hand impatiently. "Give me the map."

Henry shook his head. "Hold on, hold on." He reached into his pocket and pulled out the crumpled map, but he angled his body away from Dagger so only he could look at it. "Okay. Um . . . yeah. I guess I misread something, but . . ."

Dagger groaned. "Clearly you can't read a map! Can you give it to me, please, so we can get to the ranger station and tell the authorities what's going on?"

Henry looked up, anger flashing in his eyes. "Hey, watch it. Give me a minute to figure things out. I want to get to the ranger station even worse than you do!"

Dagger cocked his head, raising a single eyebrow. "Do you?"

The anger in Henry's eyes intensified. "What are you trying to say?"

George grabbed my arm and shot me an alarmed look. I nodded and shrugged. I could see this conversation was turning ugly, but the sleuth in me wanted to see what Dagger and Henry would say to each other, and if it would shed any light on whether either of them was involved in whatever had happened to Caitlin.

Dagger breathed in through his nose, as if to calm himself. "I am saying," he said, "that you were the last person to see your sister. You fought with her, and you are denying it. You claim to have no idea what happened to her, yet somehow, mysteriously, her satellite phone is missing as well, so we have no way of calling in the disappearance to the authorities. And now you are leading us in circles, in the guise of getting help."

Henry's eyes widened, and he swung his leg over his bike to dismount and lunged toward Dagger. "Are you seriously saying—"

"I'm stating the facts," Dagger replied, his calm expression intact.

"Why should we trust you?" Henry asked, pointing at Dagger with the hand that still held the map. "You were up and around right after my sister disappeared—don't think I didn't notice. You gave us a fake address on your tour application—yeah, I noticed that too, dude, and I brought it up to Caitlin, but she said we needed a seventh person or they'd cancel the tour—and you've paid for everything in cash. How do we know who the heck you really are? Is your name even Dagger?"

Dagger didn't flinch. "My name is Dagger now," he said calmly.

Henry shook his head, as if trying to shake something off, and then stepped back. "If I find out you hurt her . . . ," he said in a low voice, smoothing out the map.

Dagger held out his hand again. "Give me the map, Henry."

But Henry had turned back to the map and was busy trying to follow our route with his finger. "Okay, so our campsite was here," he said, his brows furrowing. "And then I think we rode here, and . . ."

Dagger sighed quietly, seeming to register that Henry was ignoring him. Then, very calmly, he reached into a pocket on his backpack and pulled out a long, gleaming, silver blade. My heart seized.

"Let's try that again," he said, gesturing toward Henry with the knife. "Give me the map."

# CHAPTER NINE

~

# Revelations

A HORRIFIED SILENCE FELL OVER THE GROUP. Without thinking, I reached out for George's and Bess's hands; they both grabbed mine, squeezing to let me know they were just as freaked as I was.

"Please," Dagger went on, his voice just as cool and calm as always. "The map, please."

Henry shot an alarmed look at the rest of us—as if to say, *You saw that, right?*—and then held the map out to Dagger. "Knock yourself out, dude."

Dagger took the map without comment. He pushed the handle of the knife between his torso and upper arm and held it there while he used both hands to spread out the map. He didn't make another peep; didn't look at the rest of us; didn't make any move to touch the knife. At one point, he took one finger and pressed it to his lip, thinking.

"Hmmmmm," he said. "Well. Hmmmmm."

I looked at Bess and George. What was happening here? I didn't know what to think; was Dagger—or the Stranger Formerly Known as Dagger—going to kill us now? Was he just waiting to figure out where we were on the map before he gutted us like fish and buried us in the woods? I could tell from my friends' expressions that they were just as thrown by this as I was.

After what seemed like an eternity, Dagger looked up. "Very well," he said, handing the map back to Henry, who took it with the enthusiasm of someone heading to the dentist for a root canal. "I am guessing we missed a turn about eight miles back. The map is a bit confusing, but we do not cross the river on this road. We need to turn off to a smaller path, then cross the river, then turn again."

He grabbed the knife and slipped it into his backpack, then walked back to his bike and set it up to mount.

Henry looked at the four of us girls; we stared, bewildered, back at him.

"Um," said Henry, straightening up, "you going to kill us now, dude?"

I cringed. Not how I would have put the question. But Dagger looked mystified as he turned back to Henry.

"What do you mean? I'm ready to continue on our way."

Henry stood even straighter. "You just pulled a knife on me, man!"

Dagger frowned at him. "What, this?" he asked, pulling the knife back out of his backpack and waving it in our direction. All five of us took a step back.

"That's the one," I said. "Dagger, why do you have a weapon?"

Dagger laughed, looking fondly at his knife. "This isn't a weapon!" he said. "I always bring my knife on hikes or camping trips. It's extremely helpful for cutting through brush, or chopping food, or in a pinch, dealing with hostile wildlife."

Henry raised his eyebrows. "Like me?" he asked.

Dagger looked at him, clearly not following.

"You pulled that knife on me," Henry said. "Don't tell me there was an angry bear behind me. You used that knife to threaten me into giving you the map."

Dagger shrugged, putting the knife back in his pack again. "Perhaps I did," he admitted. "You were frustrating me, being unreasonable. You're coleading a bike tour, yet you don't know how to read a map. I lost my patience." He paused, looking at our unsure faces. "Oh, come on. I promise you I'm not a threat to any of you. Does someone else want to take the knife?"

"Yeah," said Henry, reaching out his hands. "I'll take it."

Before I could even think through what a potentially bad idea that was—Henry being one of my two main suspects for sabotaging the trip and being behind Caitlin's disappearance—Zoe spoke up.

"I'll take it," she said, stepping forward and carefully taking the knife from Dagger. "Now, if you boys are finished swiping at each other like a couple of cranky bears, can we get back on the road? Some of us are still worried about Caitlin."

We all quickly obeyed, jumping back on our bikes and falling into formation behind Dagger now. I groaned inwardly at the thought of retracing our steps, but I held out hope that this would bring us to the ranger station—and help for all of us.

As we rounded a curve back in the direction we'd come, I found myself next to Zoe.

"Good thinking," I whispered to her, "getting the knife away from the boys. I don't quite trust either of them."

Zoe nodded grimly. "They both had the opportunity to hurt Caitlin, I know. But it's worse than you think," she whispered back. "I was talking to Dagger yesterday at lunch when no one was around. He was telling me he used to be homeless; he says he had some major issues and did all sorts of things he's not proud of. Like spending some time in jail."

I frowned. "But if it's in his past, like he says, then he isn't necessarily a threat. Did he mention anything specific?"

Zoe shook her head, then pursed her lips. "No, he didn't mention anything. It's more of just a feeling I get . . . like he's always sneaking up behind me, or something."

I shrugged, not wanting to let on that Dagger had spooked me on more than one occasion too.

I pedaled even harder. We couldn't get to the ranger station fast enough.

Four hours later the midday sun beat down unmercifully, making our group even more miserable than we already felt—which was saying something.

We were hopelessly lost. Dagger's "course correction" didn't lead to the river, and since then, each one of us had taken a turn trying to read the map and lead us in the right direction. But we had no idea where we were anymore; nothing we saw seemed to match up to any place on the map. I was beginning to worry that we'd wandered so far that we weren't even on the map anymore.

Which meant we were even farther from civilization. And even farther from the ranger station.

"We need to stop!" Zoe shouted from the back of the pack, and everyone groaned, but we still dutifully pulled over.

"This route isn't right either," she went on, although she really didn't have to say it out loud; we were all thinking it. If George had been correct in reading where we were, we would have passed a picnic area along this path. But we'd been riding for an hour and passed nothing. Now we were in a heavily forested area. Deep woods flanked the path on either side.

"Guys, I'm going to say it," Bess spoke up. She looked miserable; sweaty-faced and sunburned, deep lines of concern etched on her face. The Bess I was facing now was a far cry from the cheery, dimpled Bess I was accustomed to in "real" life. But the adventures of the day hadn't treated any of us well. "We're lost."

George fished out the map from her pocket.

"Don't even bother," said Henry, wiping the sweat off his face with the bottom of his shirt. "We're so turned around, that thing is useless."

Dagger turned to him. "And whose fault is it that we're so turned around?"

Henry sat up in his seat, turning on Dagger. "Whose fault? I tried my best here, okay? You took a turn reading the map wrong too, if I recall."

"The difference is, I'm not one of the leaders of this trip."

Henry turned pink and shoved a finger toward Dagger as though he were going to shout something back, but Zoe cut him off.

"You guys both got us lost, okay? You were both trying to be king of the mountain or whatever, and neither one of you handed off the map until we were good and lost already. I can't believe this!"

"Like you were so helpful!" Henry spat, turning on Zoe. "All you've done since we left the inn is complain! Why are you even on this tour?"

"Guys!" Bess cried, holding up her hands in a big

truce sign. "Who cares whose fault it is? Have you for-gotten that Caitlin is still missing? Every hour we sit here yelling at each other about it is another hour that she doesn't get help!"

Bess's pronouncement was greeted by a shamed silence. After a minute or so, Zoe cocked her head.

"Do you guys hear that?"

I tried to focus, but I couldn't hear anything. Maybe I was too zonked by the ride.

"It's, like, burbling," George said, looking into the trees on the right side of the road.

"I think it's a stream," Zoe said.

Henry let out a sigh of relief. "Well, that's some-thing," he said, dismounting from his bike and grab-bing his water bottle off the underside of his seat. "We can at least take a break and refill. I do have water purification tablets in my pack. Maybe we can even take a dip, if it's deep enough."

"Yes," Dagger agreed, climbing off his bike too. "Let's take a break and regroup. Then we can talk about what to do."

We left our bikes on the roadside and followed Zoe through the trees into the woods. It took a few minutes, but soon we found ourselves on the bank of a clear, bubbling stream, just deep enough for wading. We all eagerly refilled our water bottles. Henry pulled off his sneakers and waded in. After I'd wandered into the woods to answer the call of nature, I came back out and took off my shoes too. When I dunked my toes in, I gasped—the water was cold enough to take your breath away. But it felt kind of good after the hot sun. I waded in a little deeper, then splashed some water on my face.

Bess, George, Dagger, and Zoe had all dispersed, either using the bathroom or resting in the woods or filling their bottles a distance away, so I found myself alone with Henry.

"I just can't stop thinking about my sister," he said in a quiet voice, before I could say anything.

"I'm sure we'll find her," I said, trying to look optimistic, though it was getting harder and harder as the day went on.

Henry nodded. "I hope so. I keep thinking—what

if she just wandered off to, like, see a different part of the lake or something, but then she came back and we weren't there?"

I raised an eyebrow. "Henry, are you sure you two didn't fight before she disappeared?"

Henry sighed and shook his head. "For the last time, we didn't. But, you know—Caitlin gets mad at me a lot. She always says she feels like she has to work so hard for everything, and I just kind of bob along in her current, you know? We fought a lot before we left for the tour, honestly, because she felt like I wasn't pulling my weight."

I wasn't sure what to say to that. "It sounds like you guys are really different."

Henry nodded. "We are."

"But if you guys didn't fight, why would she just run off like that? Dagger said—"

"Dagger's an idiot!" Henry suddenly burst out, poking his finger in my face. "Seriously! You believe that guy?"

I stared at Henry, trying to remain calm. "I have

no reason not to," I said quietly. "Do you think he has a reason to lie about you and Caitlin fighting?"

Henry shook his head, running his hands over his face. "I don't know. I don't know anything. I just so want this all to be over."

I nodded. "Me too."

"Auuuuuughhh! No!"

A scream suddenly cut through the afternoon stillness, exploding from the direction of the road. It was female—Zoe? Henry and I looked at each other briefly and then splashed out of the stream and up onto the bank. We didn't bother to put our shoes back on as we thundered through the trees, trailing Bess, with George close behind.

"What happened?" Bess cried as she left the trees.

Zoe didn't answer in words; she just gestured to the side of the road, where our bikes lay, awaiting our return.

Every single tire on every bike had been slashed.

~

# CHAPTER TEN

# Another Long Night

AS WE ALL STOOD STARING AT THE BIKES, openmouthed, Dagger stepped out of the trees.

"You!" Henry screamed, rushing toward him. "You did this! You have a knife!"

Dagger looked confused. "I did what? I—" Then he spotted the bikes. "Oh dear."

"Oh dear?" Henry mocked, getting up in Dagger's face. "Oh dear? What kind of reaction is that? Either you did this, or you're some kind of sociopath!"

Dagger shook his head. "I'm not a sociopath," he said. "I'm just in a constantly balanced state because of my meditation. I am as upset about this as you are, I assure you. But I don't see the benefit of yelling and screaming about it."

Henry stuck a finger in Dagger's face. "Give me one good reason to believe you didn't do this," he said.

Dagger smirked. "Because I don't have the knife anymore?"

Oh, right. I had actually forgotten that too. All eyes turned to Zoe, who was crouching over her bike like it was her injured child.

She glanced up and seemed after a moment to follow what we were all thinking. "You think I did this?" she asked. "Are you kidding? Of the six of us, who do you think is most eager to get back to electricity and running water?"

She had a point there. But George didn't seem totally convinced. "Where is the knife, Zoe?"

Zoe frowned. "It's still in my pack. Look." She went over and grabbed her backpack, then unzipped the main compartment. She had to pull out a lot of clothes and toiletries to show it to us. "It's right where

I put it when I got it. If I'd used it to slash those tires, it would be on top, no?"

"Unless you knew we were going to ask," I pointed out, "and buried it back under all your clothes to look less guilty."

Zoe narrowed her eyes at me. "I did not do this," she said. "Fingerprint me if you want. But listen . . . we can't deny it anymore: Someone in this group is working against us."

"That's right," I said shakily. It was hard to say out loud—because the thought terrified me—but there was no way a stranger had done this to our bikes. "I didn't want to believe this, but it has to be true: Someone here is the culprit behind the tires and the tents and the missing food—and probably knows what happened to Caitlin."

Everyone looked at one another uncomfortably, but no one refuted what Zoe or I had said.

After a second Dagger spoke, his voice a low rumble. "Only one person in this group had any motivation to hurt Caitlin," he pointed out. "And that would be Henry. We all witnessed them arguing briefly at dinner, and they had a much more serious argument right before she disappeared."

Henry groaned. "Yeah, look, Caitlin and I argued sometimes. But I'm not the one with the knife and the fake name. How about we start with that?"

"Fine. My real name is Robert," Dagger said mildly. "Way back when, I was a very different person than I am today. I did some things I'm not exactly . . . proud of. Found myself behind bars at one point." He took a breath and continued. "A few years ago, I was coming out of a very difficult time and decided to start my life over. So I chose the name I always wanted. Dagger—it sounds very powerful, no?" He stepped closer to Henry. "Can I ask you a question? Why do you insist that you didn't fight with Caitlin before she disappeared?"

Henry glared at him. "Because I did not fight—"

"What were you involved in," Dagger went on, "that disturbed her so much? What was the text message—"

Henry suddenly leaped at Dagger, grabbing his shirt. "Caitlin doesn't approve of anything I do," he said in a gravelly voice. "Okay? I don't know what you're talking about. But she would snipe at me constantly."

Dagger stared at him warily but didn't say more. After a few seconds Henry let him go. We were all silent for a few minutes, not knowing what to say. The afternoon sun pounded down on us, and I remembered my shoes and gear were still by the stream. Not that it mattered. We weren't going anywhere, at least not via bike.

"Look, we can't turn on each other now," George said. "In a few hours it will be dark. We're lost in the woods without food, and Henry's sister is still missing. What will we do?"

Everyone was quiet. From the expressions we wore, I think we were all running through possibilities in our heads, but nobody wanted to voice our options, because they were all terrible. Stay here with no supplies? Just start walking and hope we found civilization before we all starved?

Finally Henry spoke up. "I'd like to suggest a plan," he said.

"Go ahead," said Zoe.

Henry took a deep breath, as though he were bracing himself for our reactions. "Me and Dagger take the map and try to hike to the ranger station. Failing that, maybe we would at least find an area with cell service."

George shook her head. "I thought this entire area had no cell service," she said. "I mean, I haven't gotten a single message since we've been here."

Henry nodded. "Yeah, I know, it's very sketchy out here, but there are a few places where you can get a bar or two of service," he said. "I got a couple of messages yesterday. So if we can just find one of those places, maybe we can make a call."

Suddenly Zoe squealed. "Wait a minute. If you and Dagger leave, that means you're leaving us girls here alone? In the woods? With no food, and when it's probably one of you guys who's been harassing us this whole time?"

Henry looked at Dagger, and Dagger looked back warily.

Suddenly George spoke up. "That's what makes it the perfect plan," she said. "Don't you see? Dagger and

Henry go together; they'll keep each other honest. If one of them tries anything, the other will squelch it right away."

"Yeah, or the bad guy kills the good one and then circles back to kill us," Zoe pointed out, shooting George a skeptical look.

Henry sighed. "Do you have a better plan?" he asked. "Maybe we should all stay here and sleep with one eye open until we starve or whoever's doing this stuff shows himself? I don't think so. My sister is still missing! We have to do something."

Zoe sighed. George, Bess, and I all shared a sympathetic glance.

"All right," said Bess. "All in favor of Henry's plan?"

Dagger raised his hand right away. Then George and me, then Bess, and then finally Zoe.

"You guys better walk fast," she said, still not looking at all happy about this.

It wasn't raining—in fact, there wasn't a cloud in the sky—but Zoe insisted she still wanted "some kind of shelter," so we used her tent as a tarp, stringing it between trees as Caitlin and Henry had done the night before. That at least gave us enough space to set up our sleeping bags beneath, and sleep without someone's knees in our back.

The woods felt eerily silent once the boys had gone. We did our best to fill the silence with idle chatter; Bess and Zoe spent an hour breaking down each designer's chances on *Project Runway*, and for once George actually sat and listened, and even put in a few comments here and there. After dinner—kind of a depressing meal of protein bar chunks, wild blackberries, chestnuts, and dandelion greens—Zoe insisted that we have a karaoke competition. At first I felt kind of ridiculous, belting out a Katy Perry song to the silent pine trees, but after we got going, I had to admit that it was really fun and helped us use up the manic energy we were all feeling. George sang a One Direction tune that Bess was shocked she even knew, and that led to a bubbly conversation about pop music and some pretty funny jokes about boy bands from Zoe. We kept talking and laughing until the moon was high in the sky, and then finally our constant yawning made it hard to ignore the obvious.

"I guess we should really go to sleep," Zoe said, looking nervously out into the dark. "Can't put it off forever."

We all agreed—we were too tired to argue. We set up our sleeping bags in a cross shape, with our heads at the center. Nobody said anything, but I think we were all thinking that it would be impossible to disturb one of us without the rest of us waking up too. Safety in numbers. It was all we had.

For a few minutes we all just lay there. Zoe had a flashlight, and she said she knew she should turn it off to conserve the batteries, but she didn't want to just yet.

"Hey, cuz?" Bess said sleepily.

"Yeah," said George. She sounded tense, and I wondered if, like me, she was thinking about whether she'd actually get to sleep.

"I'm really sorry about how I acted at the beginning of this trip," Bess said. "I thought I was just teasing, but you're right—this was your big thing. I'm sorry if I made you feel bad about it."

"It's cool, cuz," George replied. "And for the record? For like a minute? While we were decorating the cupcakes with edible glitter? I kind of had fun at your makeover party."

"I hate it when we fight," Bess added. "George, you'll always be my BCF. Best Cousin Forever."

"Likewise."

"Well, good night, guys—I should probably turn this off," Zoe said, flicking off the flashlight. As feeble as the tiny beam had been against the huge woods, I was still unprepared for the darkness when it was off. It felt like we were trapped in a black velvet cloud. I raised my hand in front of my face but still couldn't see it. Clouds must have been covering the moon.

As tired as I was, my mind was still racing in too many different directions to fall asleep just yet. I kept thinking over the events of the day, all leading to one big question: Whodunit? Henry or Dagger?

Dagger was right that Henry had the only motive;

but at the same time, Henry seemed so doofy and clueless, it was hard to imagine him as a criminal. Except, of course, when he'd lunged at Dagger after he asked him about the fight—that was scary. But on the other hand, we still didn't know Dagger's real full name—awfully convenient for someone planning to commit a crime. And he had a pretty huge knife, as much as he tried to insist it was a totally reasonable object to bring camping. But on the other hand . . .

I yawned and closed my eyes. Just for a minute . . .

When I woke up, it was still pitch-black and silent. *Go back to sleep*, I told myself immediately. *Wait till it's light.* But my bladder would not listen. I squirmed in my sleeping bag, urging myself to hold it for just a little while—just until it was light! Which might only be an hour or two.

But it quickly became obvious to me that that was not an option. I had to get up to find a place to relieve myself, and I had to do it now.

I sat up in my sleeping bag and scanned the area

outside our tent. Blackness. Nothing. But just as I was forcing myself to squirm out of the bag, I heard movement.

Zoe. She sat up too, looking sleepy.

"I have to go so bad," she whispered. "I've been holding it for an hour. Should we go together?"

"Oh, gosh, yes," I said breathlessly, unable to contain my relief. "I don't want to be a wimp, but . . . safety in numbers!"

Zoe smiled and we got out of our sleeping bags, then slipped out of the shelter with Bess and George still fast asleep. Zoe shone the flashlight at the trees. It should have made me feel safer, but instead it just seemed to emphasize how dark the woods were outside its feeble beam.

"There are some good privacy trees over here, I think," Zoe whispered, leading me back toward the stream. "You take the tall one over there. I'm going to go nearer to the stream. Are you okay if I take the flashlight?"

"Sure," I whispered, thinking how I kind of liked

Zoe now that I'd gotten to know her. "You'll come back when you're done?"

"Of course. We'll walk back to the tent together." Zoe walked away through the trees, leaving me in privacy.

I had never felt so relieved to take care of business and get back to bed. I stood by my tree, waiting for Zoe to come back and pick me up, but all was silent over by the stream. I figured maybe nervousness was getting the better of her, and tried to be patient.

How long had it been? It felt like five minutes or more, but surely it hadn't really been that long? If Zoe was having some kind of trouble she'd tell me, right? She knew I was waiting . . . tense . . . alone . . . in the dark . . .

"Auuuuuughh!"

The scream sliced the air like a knife—unmistakably Zoe's. I felt my insides wrench. Barely a second later, I heard the second voice.

"Gotcha!"

My lungs turned to ice.

Henry!

# CHAPTER ELEVEN

# A Midnight Visitor

"RUN, NANCY!" I HEARD ZOE YELL—followed closely by another scream. Adrenaline flooded my senses, and I could feel my heart pounding in my ears. *I have to run*, I thought, *but where?* I could barely see my hand in front of my face, and who knew where we were, besides "in the woods"?

Then I heard footsteps coming through the trees, and my instincts took over. I ran. I scuttled between trees and through brush, I tripped over logs and got up and kept going. I skinned my knees and elbows but barely felt it—I knew I just had to keep running. My life depended on it. It had to be Henry behind me, and he knew I was there, and there was no way he was running after me just to chat.

After a few minutes the footsteps behind me faded away. Had I lost him? I crashed through some bushes and reached the stream. My eyes had adjusted to the night by then, more or less—there was a sliver of moon high in the sky, and it gave me just enough light to see a few feet ahead of me. I stopped and tried to listen, but it was hard to hear anything over the blood rushing in my ears and the crazy thudding of my heart.

Something moved through the brush near the campsite, coming in my direction. Henry was still behind me—if I didn't move, he'd catch me soon. I gasped for air, trying to catch my breath and make some kind of plan. The stream burbled and poured over rocks and boulders. As I watched the water flow, I remembered something I'd read once in a book: If you're being followed and you walk through a river or stream, you leave no trace behind. No footsteps, no scent for dogs to pick up. I took a deep breath and plunged my feet into the freezing-cold water.

Immediately my ankles ached from the cold, but I didn't have time to whine about it. As quietly yet quickly as I could, I made my way over the rocks downstream. I kept going for what seemed like hours but may have only been minutes. Every so often I could hear something moving in the woods and my heart seemed to stop; I never knew whether it was just wildlife moving around . . . or Henry.

Henry. So it was him. Did that mean he'd actually done something to hurt his sister? He must have; that's why he'd led us in circles through the woods, to keep us from telling anyone. And now he'd come back to get us, I realized with a gulp. I remembered Zoe's terrified screams and shuddered. Then I thought of Bess and George, how I'd left them asleep under the tent. Were they still safe? Had Henry found them as well? What did he plan to do to all of us?

After a while, the stream bent around a curve, and then I could see the lake shimmering below in the moonlight. Mystic Lake—the stream must empty into it. The sight of the lake we'd been biking around all this time gave me hope somehow, and that hope increased when I got a little closer and could make out a small dock jutting out from the bank—with a canoe tied up to the side.

A canoe. I'd gone canoeing a few times in Girl Scouts. I was terrible at steering, but at least I could keep the vessel afloat (unlike Bess, whose canoe had capsized somehow, so she'd ended up in the water). And if I could paddle out into the lake, I'd be safe— unless Henry was a champion swimmer, he couldn't come after me.

I ran through the stream, up onto the bank to the dock. My feet made splashing sounds in the water, giving away my location to anyone listening, but I didn't care. As I scrambled down the dock toward the canoe, I heard them again: footsteps. Now he was crashing through the trees just a quick run away; soon he'd reach the edge of the trees, and then he'd surely see me, if he hadn't already.

I dove into the canoe, rocking it terribly and making even more of a racket. I started unwinding the rope that fixed the canoe to the dock. Focus . . . focus . . . I heard someone just yards away at the edge of the woods. With trembling fingers, I unwound the last piece and pushed as hard as I could away from the dock.

Paddle. Paddle. I wasn't exactly an expert canoer, but I knew that the faster I got away from the dock, the less likely Henry was to come after me. I forced myself not to look back, just to keep paddling, focusing on a spot in the middle of the lake that was shining by the light of the moon. If I could just get there . . .

*Splash. Splash.* The paddle cut into the water, over and over again. An owl hooted somewhere, and I took in breath after desperate breath of night air. Finally I looked up and saw that I was nearly at the point I was aiming for—much too far for someone to swim after me. Only then did I allow myself to look back.

My blood chilled. I was far enough away, and the moonlight was weak enough so that I could only make out a shadowy figure on the edge of the dock. The figure saw me, though. As I pulled the paddle back through the water, it raised its hand, as if to wave.

Gulp.

I was safe now—or was I? The figure couldn't come after me, but I was also completely vulnerable. I realized now that we were in a small pocket of the huge, sprawling Mystic Lake; you could probably circle the whole area in about an hour. And he could track my movements wherever I went; if I began paddling for the far bank, for example, he could easily try to outrun me on foot and meet me there.

What now?

I pulled out my phone, knowing it was a long shot, and I was right: no service. Trying to calm my still-pounding heart, I took a deep breath and looked around. Then another terrible thought occurred to me.

If Henry was behind everything and he'd come back here, what did he do to Dagger?

I shuddered. I hoped the meditation-loving nature enthusiast was still alive.

Then I caught sight of something across the water,

not far from the direction I'd come from. It was a small wooden structure—a shed—no, a cabin. I felt a tingle of hope in my chest. There were no lights on, but if I could get over there, maybe there would be someone inside, sleeping—or even just a landline I could use. Or a bike. Or a car. (George once taught Bess and me how to hot-wire a car—for emergencies—and I was not above using that information in a pinch.)

If I could get to that cabin, maybe I could find a way to get help.

I started paddling, at first trying to be stealthy about it, then quickly realizing how ridiculous that was and just trying to move the canoe as fast as I possibly could. After what felt like an eternity, I was close enough to see that the cabin had a small dock. About a dozen yards away I gave up paddling and just jumped into the lake, swimming wildly for a ladder on the dock's side. I was desperate. I knew seconds counted if I was going to get help before Henry found me.

I scrambled up onto the dock and ran down toward the cabin, soaking wet, cold, and dripping. The closer I got, the more clear it became that the cabin was unin-habited. There was no car parked nearby, no bike. The windows were dark; no sign of life inside.

Still, I was quiet as I snuck up on the small porch. I didn't want to startle anyone inside. And if Henry was nearby but somehow hadn't spotted me yet, I didn't want to attract any attention.

I felt for the doorknob and automatically tried to turn it. The latch easily gave way and the door pushed open. *Really?* I wondered, staring at the tiny sliver of the dark front room that was now exposed. *Maybe we're so far out in the wilderness, they don't think it's necessary to lock their door?*

I stepped inside. If they didn't lock their door, they must have a phone for emergencies—right? That was just good common sense. I could only hope they had a landline.

I looked around. There was just enough moonlight reflecting off the lake and through the window for me to see that I was inside a small kitchen. There was a sink below a window, a small fridge, and a two-burner stove. My stomach rumbled, and it occurred to me that there might be some food in the cabin, but first I wanted to find a phone.

There was a door off to the right that seemed to lead to a small living room. I walked toward it, and just as I passed over the threshold I was suddenly blinded as the lights in the living room went on.

I felt a chill go up my spine. I blinked, trying to make my eyes focus in the sudden bright light. I could just make out two figures sitting on a small plaid couch.

"Hello, Nancy," said a familiar voice.

# CHAPTER TWELVE

~

# Cabin in the Woods

IT SEEMED LIKE IT TOOK FOREVER FOR MY eyes to focus. When they finally did, I wondered if I was seeing things.

"Caitlin!"

My tour leader smiled, tossing her long blond ponytail. "Aren't you a clever little thing, Nancy? Too nosy for your own good. I'd say you're a kindred spirit, a future overachiever, but I wouldn't want to wish my life on you."

I shook my head, then turned to the figure sitting next to Caitlin. Wait a minute.

"Zoe? How did you get here so quickly?"

Caitlin laughed, and Zoe smiled as she looked from Caitlin to me. "I knew a shortcut. And, honey? You're not exactly ready for the Olympic canoeing team. You never did catch on that we know each other, did you?" Zoe asked me, a faint smile on her face. "So maybe it would have taken you a little longer to figure out everything. But we couldn't be too careful."

Figure out everything . . . wait. "You faked your own disappearance?" I asked, turning back to Caitlin. "But—why? Your life seems . . . perfect."

Caitlin rolled her eyes at me.

"What?" I asked. "You graduated with this crazy high GPA and you're going to Yale on scholarship in the fall!"

Caitlin shrugged one shoulder. "It's not like I wanted to give all that up," she said, sniffing. "I just needed a break, okay?"

"From?" I asked, still utterly confused.

"From the sheer effort of being me!" she exclaimed. "Working so hard all the time. Being perfect. Making sure everything goes according to plan. Taking care of my parents, making them happy, so my brother has time to loaf around and do whatever he does." She sighed and blew some hair out of her face.

Zoe elbowed her. "I think it's all too clear what he does," she said, making a face, then laughing.

Caitlin groaned. "Oh, don't remind me."

So Henry . . . I struggled to understand. "Wait a minute. Was Henry in on it?"

Caitlin laughed. "As if! No, Henry was part of the reason I needed to get away."

I raised my eyebrows, silently asking for more information.

She sighed. "Listen. Henry and I are twins, but we couldn't be more different. Since we were tiny babies, it's always been this way: I'm the good one. He's the lazy one. But the thing is, everyone loves Henry, so it doesn't matter."

"And that makes you . . . mad?" I asked.

Caitlin glared at me. "Of course it makes me mad! Wouldn't it make you mad?" She shook her head. "All through school, I'm up late studying, he's up watching dumb videos on his computer and hanging out with his stupid friends. I work all summer to save money for college, he goes to surfing camp on my parents' dime. And now I'm going to Yale on scholarship and paying for books myself, but he somehow convinced our parents to bankroll his six-month backpacking trip through Europe. How does he do it? And why can't I get away with it?" She sighed again.

"So your coleading this tour with him and disappearing," I began, "was your way of framing him? To get revenge?"

Caitlin stood up, holding out one hand to me. "No, no. I mean, not exactly. I wanted it to look like he did it for a while. I wanted him to feel bad, to wish he'd treated me better." She paused. "What happened was, last spring I went to this weeklong camp for high-achieving girls. And that's where I met Zoe."

I glanced at Zoe, surprised. She smirked.

"Don't look so shocked, Nancy. I actually started my first business—a manicure salon that makes house calls—when I was just fifteen. I really don't like camping, but that doesn't mean I'm totally useless."

I nodded. "Of course not. Um . . . how does that relate to Caitlin disappearing?"

Caitlin smiled at Zoe. "Well, Zoe here, she saw how crazed I was about everything and how hard I had to work and how miserable I was. She was the one who told me, 'Honey, you need a break. Life doesn't have to be this hard.' So I started opening up to her, talking about my life and my family and everything that's going on. She and I started talking about how I could get a few days off for myself. So when my parents asked me if I'd let Henry colead this bike tour with me—since I needed a coleader anyway—I said sure. And as I was planning it, and Henry wasn't helping me one bit, I started thinking, Hey, what if there were a way to use this tour to show everyone what a screwup Henry is? And in the process, I realized, I could get a little vacation."

I took a deep breath. "A vacation?" I asked. "That's what you're calling your . . . disappearance?"

Caitlin nodded. "I was going to come back in a few days. Claim I'd bumped my head on my way back from the bathroom, got a little disoriented, wandered off, then lived off the land until I could find the ranger station." She smiled. "Genius."

I frowned. "And the satellite phone? The missing tents, the food?"

Her grin widened. "I took them all and stashed them in a hiding spot in the woods. When I left, I wanted to make the tour look like a total disaster. Look how useless Henry is! He doesn't even know where the satellite phone is! I even spent two weeks mocking up a fake map of the Mystic Lake area, so you guys could get completely, hopelessly lost before you'd find help. Then I slashed all your tires at the stream, just to drive the subject home."

I couldn't believe all this. "What about your job with Adventures and Company?" I asked. "When the tents went missing, Henry said something about you wanting them to hire you next summer."

Caitlin laughed. "Oh, I couldn't care less," she said.

"I'm sure an all-star student like me won't have any trouble finding a job. But I wanted Henry to feel good and guilty when he'd completely messed up this tour, in addition to losing his sister."

I shook my head. "Do you realize that Henry and Dagger have been fighting each other all day about who had something to do with your disappearance?"

Caitlin laughed, looking delighted, and turned to Zoe.

"It's true," Zoe said. "Henry came up with this whole theory about how Dagger used a fake name to kidnap you or something. I kind of fed into it. And it just so happens that Dagger travels with this crazy knife. Henry almost got into a fistfight with him over it."

Caitlin's cheeks turned a tiny bit pink. "Wow," she said. "That's kind of sweet. I didn't know Henry had it in him."

So Dagger really had nothing to do with it—he was just in the wrong place at the wrong time.

I was silent, my mind reeling. Something was still

nagging at me. "Did you and Henry really fight right before you disappeared?" I asked. "Something about a text message?"

"Ah, the text message fight!" Caitlin said with a laugh. "Yeah. I may have neglected to mention—as if I didn't have enough ammunition to set this whole plan in motion—about two weeks before we left, I intercepted a text message to Henry talking about the insane amount of debt he's racked up gambling."

"Gambling?" I asked.

"Betting on horses at the racetrack." Caitlin nodded. "He owes like, five or six grand at this point. So stupid. Anyway, I purposely picked a fight with him before I took off. We both woke up early that morning, and I wanted someone to hear us arguing, to place more suspicion on him. But when I tried to yell at him about this text message, the blockhead barely responded. He yelled back a couple of times and then was like, 'Whatever, Cait.'" She paused, fuming. "Can you believe that?" she asked. "I mean, he's too lazy to fight properly."

I nodded. It was all coming together in my head, forming into a clearer picture. Dagger had heard them fighting—but Henry probably felt guilty about his gambling debts, which might be why he'd yelled at Dagger for bringing it up.

Henry really had nothing to do with Caitlin's disappearance, or the other sabotage of the tour. He was guilty only of being a lazy, somewhat troublemaking brother.

And Dagger had nothing to do with any of this. He only had the misfortune of having changed his name, liking early morning meditation, and carrying a hunting knife.

Now I became dimly aware of both Zoe and Caitlin staring at me.

"It was the perfect plan," Zoe said.

Caitlin nodded. "The only problem," she added, not taking her eyes off me, "was you."

"Me?" I asked.

Caitlin nodded again. "You wouldn't shut up. You kept asking questions. Who did this, who did that, did you really see this, what about this." She scowled. "You were kind of going in circles so far, true, but sooner or later you were going to figure this out." She looked at me with what seemed like grudging admiration. "I'm an overachiever too—I know the type," she said.

I swallowed, not sure what to say. "Thanks?"

Zoe nodded. "Before Cait took off, she left me a little present. A satellite phone of my very own. This allowed me to get in touch with her if anything came up. So today, when we stopped by the stream, I went into the woods and called her. I told her you were asking too many questions; something had to be done. We decided to grab you tonight."

Caitlin tilted her head to the side. "Unfortunately, you were a much faster runner than we thought," she said with a sigh. "And once you got to that canoe out on the lake, we knew it was just a matter of time till you found my little hideout here."

I shook my head. "But wait—I heard Henry saying 'Gotcha' right after you screamed, Zoe," I pointed out. "Where did that come from? And why?"

Caitlin smirked. "Show her, Zoe," she said, gesturing to Zoe's pocket.

With a smug grin, Zoe pulled out her smartphone and clicked on the music icon. Then she selected an MP3 and hit play.

"Gotcha, sis! April Fool's! Ha-ha, you have to admit, that was a good one." Henry.

Caitlin giggled. "It's amazing what you can get someone saying when you record their conversations with you for, like, three months. I knew it would come in handy sometime."

My head was still spinning. "But why?" I asked. "If you were just getting me out of the way . . . "

"Our plan was to conk you over the head with a rock and drag you to the shed outside before you woke up," Caitlin explained.

I stared at her, waiting for some sign that she was kidding, but she gave none.

"We'd keep you here until I was ready to give myself up. But just in case you got loose, we figured it was a good idea for you to think that Henry was behind the whole thing. You know, in case you made it to the ranger station."

"Speaking of which . . ." Zoe reached back for something leaning against the coffee table, then held it up. It was a huge, rusty shovel. "We should probably go ahead and introduce you to your home away from home for the next few days." She raised the shovel menacingly.

# CHAPTER THIRTEEN

~

# Desperate

"WHAT DO YOU MEAN?" I ASKED, SHRINKING back. *What would these girls do to me?* I wondered. *Would they really hurt me?*

Caitlin took in a deep breath through her nose. "I'm not quite ready for the game to be over," she said. "This is supposed to be my vacation by the lake, and as you can see, I still have a bunch of books to get through." She gestured to the coffee table, where, indeed, about five or six romance paperbacks were piled up. "We're borrowing this cabin without the owner's knowledge, but we found a shed out there that has no windows and a padlock on the door—it seems like a pretty good place to keep a nosy wannabe detective."

I shook my head. "Come on, guys," I said, trying to paste on my most we're-all-friends-here type smile. "You don't have to lock me up! I mean, you hit the nail on the head, Caitlin—I'm a total overachiever, just like you. I could sooo use some time by the lake myself. I get what you're doing now, really, and I wouldn't tell anybody."

Caitlin glanced at Zoe, who shook her head. Caitlin smirked. "That's cool, Drama Club," she said, gesturing to the shovel. Zoe again raised it in the air. I instinctively backed away. "But I'm not quite convinced by your performance."

I swallowed hard. A plan was taking shape in the back of my mind, but I cowered down and made my voice high and desperate. "Please, guys," I said, "don't make me—"

The girls swooped down on me, each grabbing me by an arm, and dragged me toward the door of the cabin. Zoe was holding the shovel in her other hand,

and when we reached the porch, I was able to twist my right hand out of her grasp and reach up to pinch her armpit—hard. She dropped the shovel on her foot, letting out a shrill cry, and Caitlin loosened her grip just enough for me to pull away.

I ran off the porch, down the path to the lake, and out onto the dock.

By the time I dove in and started swimming for the canoe, they were following me, but neither one was brave enough to dive in after me. I grabbed the canoe from where it had drifted about fifty feet out into the lake and pulled myself up and in. Then I grabbed the paddle and started paddling.

Just like before. *Don't think, just paddle.*

I went as fast as my arms could carry me.

Caitlin and Zoe dragged a rowboat down from the bank of the lake and climbed in, but luckily, I had a big head start. Out on the lake, it took me a minute to get my bearings, but I soon recognized the direction I'd come from by the pattern of the trees and the angle of the moon—as I got closer, I could see the stream I'd waded through to get to the lake. I paddled back to the dock and jumped out, hoping that the canoe's owners wouldn't mind that I hadn't bothered to tie the thing up. Terrified, I quickly glanced behind me, and, sure enough, Zoe and Caitlin were rowing furiously, getting closer and closer to the dock.

I splashed through the stream until I thought I was in the area we'd camped, and then just started screaming. "BESS! GEORGE!" I splashed up and down the bank of the stream, peeping through the trees, trying to find any sign of life. "BESS! GEORGE!"

When I'd been yelling for about two minutes, I heard Bess's voice.

"Nancy! Is that you?"

They came crashing through the woods. I ran to them like a starving man to a drumstick and threw my arms around them, letting out a moan of relief.

"Are you okay?" George asked, grabbing my face and looking into my eyes. "We heard Zoe scream. We heard her tell you to run. We were scared as anything, but then nothing happened. No one came after us. We heard footsteps all around. After a few minutes we got up and started looking for you. But there was no sign anywhere."

"It's a long story," I said, glancing back in the direction I'd come. Caitlin and Zoe would be at the dock soon, if they weren't by now. We didn't have a lot of time.

"Guys," I said to my friends, not for the first time, and probably not for the last, "we have to run!"

# CHAPTER FOURTEEN

# The Truth Comes Out

"OH MY GOSH," BESS WHISPERED, STAGGERING over a tree root and nearly falling over. "I can't believe we're still in these woods. I can't believe we're not back in River Heights by now. How far have we come?"

I inhaled a deep breath. It was morning. We'd been running, and then hiking, through the woods ever since I'd found my friends who knew how many hours before.

"We've probably walked a few miles," I said. "The problem is, we don't have any idea where we are, or where we're going. So we're probably walking in circles."

"I'm so hungry," George moaned. "I haven't even

seen any blackberries in this part of the woods. I'm about to eat some bark."

"Don't do it," I said. "It would play into Caitlin's plan if we ended up poisoning ourselves out here."

George grunted her assent.

I'd explained everything that had happened to me since I'd left the tent the night before. Zoe's scream, hearing Henry's voice, and then being chased through the woods down to the canoe, as well as the whole confrontation with Zoe and Caitlin.

"I just can't believe Zoe was behind this whole thing," Bess mused. "She was a good actress. She complained about every setback—but meanwhile she had helped plan them all."

"Kind of nervy of her to bring the extra tent," George said, "when you think about it."

I nodded. "I don't think Caitlin or Zoe thought they'd ever get caught," I said. "I get the feeling Caitlin's so used to making everything go perfectly, she thought she'd get away with this, too."

"Poor Henry." Bess sighed. "I guess it's a good

thing I don't have a twin who's my opposite and who I kind of hate."

George shot her a sidelong glance. "Yeah, it's probably good we're cousins, not siblings."

Bess gave her a rueful smile.

That's when I heard something. A rumble, so familiar and yet so . . .

"A car!" I yelled, trying to track the direction it was coming from. "To the right there. Do you hear it? Just through those trees . . ."

Bess's expression looked like I'd just told her there was a million dollars on the ground, ripe for the taking. "What are we waiting for? Run!"

We ran. I'm not sure I had ever moved that fast before, or that I'll ever move that fast again. We shot through the trees and came out onto a narrow two-lane road. I could just see the taillights of a Jeep retreating into the cool dawn mist.

"WAIT!" I screamed, my feet slapping on the pavement as I ran after it. "WAIT! We need help! PLEASE!"

The Jeep had nearly disappeared around the bend. I felt hope dying in my heart. But then, at the last moment, it stopped and a moment later the passenger door opened up and a curious face popped out.

"Girls?"

"Dagger!" George cried, running at him.

The driver's-side door opened up to reveal an older man wearing a park ranger uniform. "Are you part of the bike tour group that split up yesterday?" he asked me, looking stern.

"We are," I said.

He nodded, glancing at Dagger. "Well, I have a lot of questions for you."

"Good," I said cheerfully. "I hope you have sandwiches, too."

It turned out that Henry and Dagger had found the ranger station in the middle of the night, but when they'd led the rangers back to our campsite, they'd found the empty sleeping bags and known something was wrong. After we'd told him the whole sordid story, the park ranger took us to the local police station a few miles outside Mystic Lake Park and said he was bringing together some rangers to look for Caitlin and Zoe. By that time, George and Bess and I had gobbled up some bagels ordered for us by the officers and were relaxing in a room with Henry and Dagger.

Dagger had, surprisingly, taken the news of Caitlin's faked disappearance in stride. "She's clearly out of balance, mentally," he said mildly.

Henry, on the other hand, was sitting alone in a chair by the wall, his head in his hands, looking utterly stricken.

"I knew we had our differences," he'd said a few minutes ago, speaking to the whole room, I guess. "I knew she thought I was lazy. But this is just insane. This is just . . . insane."

He'd admitted that he had some pretty serious gambling debts, and that that was why he'd denied fighting with Caitlin before she disappeared. He hadn't wanted to reveal to the rest of the group what he was really up to.

As we waited for our parents to show, the cops brought Henry back to ask him some more questions. "They've found Caitlin and Zoe," the young officer who came for Henry told the rest of us. "They were hiking along the road a few miles from the cabin you described. Some officers are bringing them in for questioning."

My stomach dropped a little. I didn't really want to look at Caitlin and Zoe as they were brought into the police station, knowing that I'd foiled their crazy plan. Actually, I wanted to be done with this whole chapter of my life. I wanted to go home, see my dad, take a bath, put on clean pj's, eat a bowl of our housekeeper Hannah's amazing fettuccine alfredo, call my boyfriend, Ned, and then collapse into my own bed.

And sleep for three days.

And never go camping again.

Before I could even express my thoughts to Bess and George, the Faynes pushed open the door to the little room we were being held in, followed by another officer.

"So we can take them, correct?" Mr. Fayne was asking. "These girls are free to go?"

"Yes, sir," the officer said with a nod.

"Oh, muffin," Mrs. Fayne cried, running straight for George. "Are you okay?"

George hugged her mom back hard. "I'm fine, Mom. Tired. And a little freaked out. But fine. I guess maybe a gift card would have been a better birthday present, huh?" she joked feebly.

But Mrs. Fayne shook her head. "Not at all, honey," she said. "I'm so sorry for you, for the way this turned out. But you're a responsible girl. This wasn't your fault."

George looked at her mom and beamed. They hugged again, and Mr. Fayne suggested, "Let's get out of here. If any happening ever called for pancakes, this is it."

I couldn't have agreed more. We said our good-byes to Dagger and were on our way.


"Omigosh, pancakes," Bess moaned an hour later, as we gobbled up our breakfast. "Food of the gods. Seriously,

George, why would you ever want to go camping or anywhere they don't have pancakes?"

George shot her cousin an annoyed look, but she soon dissolved into a smile. "Well . . . let's just say I'm done with camping for a little while. Maybe not forever. But I'm going to take a break."

I grinned at her over my orange juice. "No camping trip for your birthday next year, George?"

She shook her head. "Definitely not."

Bess raised a hand like she was in school. "Can I make a suggestion for your birthday celebration next year?" she asked.

George shot her a sideways look. "I guess . . ."

Bess grinned. "Slumber party?"

I giggled. After a moment, George chimed in too.

"Only if you'll both be there," she said with a chuckle.

We both grinned. I nodded. "Deal!"

# Dear Diary,

SO THERE YOU HAVE IT: A PERFECTIONIST pushed too far! Who knows what Caitlin would have done in order to get her little "vacation" in the woods? I'm just glad we figured out her plan before she did some real damage, not only to us, but to her brother's reputation.

And thank goodness Bess and George were there. Because in the end, there aren't many people I'd want to get stuck in the woods with besides my two best friends.